SILVER DESTINY

Silver Fox

Book One

SUSAN WARNER

SILVER DESTINY

First edition. March 21, 2019.

ISBN: 978-1-948377-31-7

Written by Susan Warner.

Chapter One

"How did I get in this situation?"

Delilah Cade looked at Peaches, the 60-pound tan and white pit bull, sitting in the back seat of her car. Somehow, Delilah had been talked into fostering Peaches for a little bit. In retrospect, she had no idea exactly how long a little bit was, but she had agreed. How could she not have? At a tent at the fair, workers had been showing off dogs that needed to be adopted. Peaches had lain on the ground, off to the side, and no one had even gone over to pet her.

When Delilah had asked the worker about her, she'd replied that Peaches was a senior dog.

She didn't move as well and had some arthritis in her hip. If Peaches didn't get adopted today, she'd probably have to be put down. With so many dogs coming in and Peaches' chance of getting adopted being so slim, they had no choice unless another agency took her or they found a foster home.

At 68, Delilah understood what it meant to be put on the side. Not that long ago, she had been thinking about taking herself somewhere out of sight so she wouldn't be a bother or a nuisance. When Delilah had gone over to pet Peaches, the dog had lifted her head and smiled. What had happened after that was all a blur. What Delilah remembered was leaving with Peaches to go to her rental in town. The shelter owner knew the address, and everyone knew she was Adam Cade's grandmother. For once in Sweet Blooms, having everyone know her name was a plus.

"No good deed goes unpunished," Delilah muttered as she reached to the back of her car and made sure Peaches was okay and still sleeping. She had bought a child monitor, with a speaker and a screen, that was supposedly good up to a quarter of a mile away. Delilah looked at the portable monitor in her purse and checked she could see and hear Peaches.

In less than five minutes, she had a meeting with Robert Parker, her new partner for the next couple of months. Like she needed that in her life. Delilah had been a widow for close to twenty years. What did she know about partnerships now?

After tucking the monitor in her purse, she left the handbag open so she could look into it. Then she went inside the Banter House restaurant, the local diner that everyone wound up at eventually. When she saw the hostess, the young lady smiled and greeted her.

"I'm here to meet Robert Parker."

The young lady nodded rather vigorously and pointed to a booth in front of them.

"Thank you." While walking toward the booth, Delilah glanced in her bag. Peaches was still asleep, thank goodness. Delilah would make her introductions and go.

As she approached, a man rose and stood by the table.

It had been a long time since a man had had enough training to stand when Delilah came to a table.

"Hello, Ms. Cade."

"I am. You are Robert Parker?"

He nodded. For a moment. she was still so shocked by his manners that she didn't comprehend why they were both standing.

"Oh, my! Please, take a seat."

"I will, after you."

Delilah thought to tell him such chivalry

wasn't necessary, but something in his tone told her this wasn't really a conversation. He would stand there all day long if need be.

She took a seat in the booth and positioned her purse on her side so she could still see the monitor. For a moment, she thought Peaches was waking up, but she was just having doggy dreams and rolled over on her side.

"So, Mr. Parker, you are probably wondering why I asked to meet you."

"No. I know why you're here."

"Well, the reason is—" As his words penetrated her consciousness, she looked at him sitting serenely across from her.

"Excuse me?"

"There's nothing to excuse," he said. "I'm aware of the issue with Pierce Morgan. I'm the one who told Adam Pierce was using inferior products and disreputable vendors. Then he asked whether I would manage the project.

I said yes. Hannah asked if I would be offended if I co-managed with someone from the company. She needed someone who represented their values and interests involved. I agreed."

Delilah listened to him itemize their meeting, and for a moment, couldn't respond. In her mind, she was strangling him. Did he have any idea how she'd tried to think of ways to tell him all the things he obviously already knew and get him to agree?

"Well, if you knew all of that then why did you agree to meet me? You could have saved us both some time," she said as politely as she could and moved to get up.

"Ms. Cade, please. I saved you some time so you wouldn't have to ask me anything. I agree to the partnership, of course. I went along with the meeting because I wanted to meet you. We're going to be working together."

"I agree we should know each other, but let's be clear. You didn't save me any time. I only have an hour at best. If you were truly going to save me the time, we'd leave now," she said sweetly.

He raised his hand. A young woman came to the table right away.

"Do you want to place an order?" she asked eagerly.

Robert smiled. "We're not staying long; two sweet teas will do for now." The waitress went off to do his bidding, not even waiting to see if Delilah wanted to order.

Delilah curled her hand on the table. This man had gotten her hackles up, and she hadn't even been around him for ten minutes. She wasn't blind. He was handsome, with his low cut salt-and-pepper hair and trimmed beard. His brown eyes had seen their share of life. One of the things she liked was his dimples.

Two of them showed up when he smiled. His dimples almost made up for the high-handed way he'd ordered for them both.

"Presumptuous, aren't you? What if I didn't drink sweet tea?" she asked.

"I would have had two teas and ordered you whatever you wanted," he said without missing a beat.

She had to admit, he wasn't what she'd been expecting. She opened her bag a little wider to ensure she could see the baby monitor. Peaches still slept. Delilah didn't want to be rude and leave, but she also didn't want to push her luck on how long the dog would sleep.

Delilah's gaze focused on Robert Parker.

"You'd like to talk, so let's begin. The hour is ticking."

"Okay." Robert grinned. "Are you single?"

Delilah couldn't control her shock.

"What kind of question is that?" she snapped.

"An important one, from where I'm sitting."

"Then I suggest you re-evaluate," she said through tight lips. Just then the waitress, all smiles, returned.

"Here are your teas," she said with a peppy little bob.

He pushed a tea toward Delilah. "Please, have some, before you decide to put me in my place."

Delilah nodded and took a sip. "Listen, Mr. Parker. I don't know if you are aware, but I'm a widow. I'm in town with my grandchildren. In fact, the project you and I will be working on is for my grandson. I don't engage in one-night stands. I'm not interested in being friends who engage in extracurricular activities, and I feel no need to keep a side piece or otherwise in the wings. I'll be working on this project with you to make sure my grandson's interests are represented. Are we clear?"

"Crystal." His smile would have melted right through her resolve if she hadn't heard a bark on the child monitor. She took a look, and sure enough, Peaches had her head up and was looking around the car. She hadn't got up yet, but Delilah knew it was only a matter of time.

"I'm so sorry. I've got to go." Delilah scooted out from the booth only to find Robert standing before her. How he'd managed to beat her out of the seat was an unknown she'd have to think about later.

"I'll see you soon, Delilah Cade."

"Yes, yes, the project is starting soon. Glad we've met and laid down some ground rules. I have to leave."

A whimper came from the monitor, and Delilah didn't even bother to pull her coat together. Instead, she rushed to the car. Peaches' nose was pressed against the window, and her breath had created a little fog on the glass. When Delilah got into the vehicle, she had to pat Peaches on the head and calm her down.

"See? I wasn't gone long, and I came right back as soon as you got up," Delilah crooned. After a couple more reassuring pats, Peaches laid back down, and Delilah turned to go home. Originally, she had come to Sweet Blooms and stayed at the bed and breakfast owned by Hannah Jenkins. After a couple of weeks, Hannah had fallen in love with Delilah's grandson, Adam Cade. When the relationship had taken off, Delilah had thought it best she had her own place. As a result, she had rented a small cottage at the edge of town.

On her drive to the cottage, she thought about Robert Parker. When was the last time she had thought about a man as a man? She knew lots of men, but they were friends or acquaintances. Robert Parker was definitely a man.

Frustrating, too, for him to have asked about her status, as if it would ever be an issue for him to worry about. Even worse: While he was a thorn used to getting his way, for a hot minute after he had smiled at her, she'd felt a spark of interest.

It wasn't lust; that was such a primitive word. The spark had said to her: *Give him a second look. Let's see if he can talk about anything interesting. Give him a chance to engage your mind.* Robert Parker didn't look like he would lack romantic partners, period. She had no interest in reliving her twenties in her mid-sixties body. She was a woman who had already known being loved by a man who adored her. Since her husband's death, she hadn't been interested in any other man.

Robert Parker sparked an interest in her. She shook her head. He seemed accustomed to getting his way, and since she had already said no, he'd find some other female who'd enjoy his attention.

She was a woman from a different time. She wasn't even sure what it meant to be in a relationship today. Peaches snored. Delilah laughed. She didn't have to worry about a relationship; she now had a four-legged child.

———

Robert pushed the two dry erase boards together. He'd been working on getting this group together for months. He wasn't concerned about the material; he knew the material. He was concerned about the audience. When he'd retired to Sweet Blooms three years ago, a bunch of "swamp men," as they were called, had lived in the nearby swamps and had only came into town to bring in crafts they'd made by hand or items their wives had made.

Most of the men were descended from local tribes that had retained some land, or they were people who had decided they wanted a different kind of life. They didn't have a lot of contact with the town, and they only brought their goods when they needed extra funds. Since Robert had come home, he had reached out to them and been their spokesperson for the last year. It was time to pull the business plan together and in action. He'd seen the way they lived, and they and their families deserved a better quality of life.

When he'd moved back to Sweet Blooms, he'd bought an old farm. At the time, he'd had no use for the property's two external buildings. One of them had had some sleeping gear in it. Two weeks later, a swamp man, bringing goods, had come to sleep over. That was when Robert had met Evan. Evan had explained the swamp men's plight, and Robert had decided what to do with the buildings. One he'd converted into three rooms in which the swamp men could stay over; the other had become a meeting and working house where the craftsmen could gather to discuss issues as well as do last minute put-together work before they dropped off their products in town.

He was setting up in the workhouse to show a proposal to the men who were coming today. To earn this trust, Robert had spent a day or two with them in their homes. He wanted to do right by them, and it gave him purpose while he was in town. He understood men who'd sacrificed for their families. After being career military, he still had the need to give back, and this opportunity allowed him to do so.

He'd also gone over his own life goals and decided how he wanted to serve and what part he wanted to play at Sweet Blooms. Setting up this guild of craftsmen allowed him the opportunity to serve, to be involved locally, and to generate income.

Thirty minutes later, the swamp men walked in. Robert had set out coffee on the side table and some biscuits as well. Doing a PowerPoint presentation wasn't going to help as most of the swamp men didn't even own computers. Instead, Robert had opted to use dry erase boards. On one, he'd written all of their names and how much money they had made in town last year. If he could streamline their production and do pickup from them as well, he could get them steady work and more income.

"Grab some food and take a seat," Robert said. He waited until everyone had settled down. "Thanks for coming. I tried to make this meeting convenient. I know a lot of you are here to drop off goods for the fair. I've been watching for the last two years, and I've seen how you all make ends meet. I'd like to suggest we build something called a guild. This guild will go to town and get requests for goods and then tell you as the orders come in what we would need. The value of this arrangment is that I can advocate for you. This means if you tell me you or your wives have specific crafts you want to sell, I'll let the buyers know and get you some sales.

A lot of you may be thinking your lives will be taken over having to make things and you won't be able to do your daily work. Let me assure you, that will not be the case. All of you produce natural goods that, for lack of better wording, tourists and city people love. You can make as much or as little as you want. I'll sit with each of you to go over the goals you want to meet.

I wrote some goals on the board. Evan needs a new generator. Case and his brother are looking for building materials for an ice house, and I hear congratulations are in order; Tom will have a new arrival come the winter."

After Tom received several pats on the back, Robert knew he had the group's interest and went on to show them what they were making and how they could earn more. He asked what concerns they had and how they wanted to address them in the guild. They went over everything from trade and barter to pricing goods.

"This has been a productive meeting. There are two items to discuss to finish up. We all have to say if we think the guild is a good idea, and if so, we'll then decide who will go to the town council and let them know there will be a new way to ask for items from us. While I put the plan together, that doesn't mean I lead it. It's your hard work, and I want you to make sure you are involved in how the guild's run."

Robert turned the meeting over to the

swamp men. They looked at one another and gathered in small groups for all of ten minutes. Evan looked around the nodding crowd before he spoke.

"We're all good that you should be the one," he said. "None of us wants to be in town that much. You did all the work, and you've spent all the time making sure we're good. You should do it."

Case raised his hand, and after Robert's nod, stood up. "What do you think the town council will do?"

"The council likes the way we bring people to the town. Almost all of our items sell out. On top of that, I'm working with Adam Cade. He's building a woodworking shop. I have some things here you can use, but when his shop is done, you'll love working there. Adam is a big name in the town, so we have lots of support."

Tom raised his hand.

"You spent a lot of time looking at the things people make, but my Sissy, she cooks. Is this going to work for her, too?"

Robert looked at the weathered man. Tom, in his late 40s, ran a small farm. With the furniture he made and his wife's cooking, they traded for their livelihood.

"I asked about the perishable goods as well. We have a following when it comes to pies. The Banter House diner in town is interested in getting baked goods—fresh and frozen—for their place."

Tom smiled and nodded before settling back in his seat.

For a while longer, they talked about transportation and communication, each man making sure he wasn't taking from the other. In some cases, Robert heard them say who would craft what so they wouldn't overlap.

Robert just looked on while they worked out details amongst themselves. He experienced more than just satisfaction that his pitch had gone well. These men reminded him of his team in the service. Although a lot of his military colleagues weren't alive anymore, he saw the same dedication and loyalty amongst the swamp men that he had with his old unit. Some hard times would be coming, but he looked forward to creating something that would stand the test of time and help these men and their families.

Chapter Two

Delilah dropped Peaches off at the groomer's. Today, she wanted to take a look around Adam's woodworking house to get an idea of what had already been done, and she wanted to walk around the land to make sure it was a good fit.

Thank goodness Delilah was an early riser. Peaches had to be dropped off at 7 a.m. and picked up promptly at 3 p.m. Every morning in Sweet Blooms, though, was a beautiful one. The sun was easy first thing, and the breeze was just right. With a blue sky 80% of the time, she could wear sundresses for eight of the twelve months in the 70-degree weather. She was in a town she grew up in, she was helping her grandson build his new life, and she was doing something in her life to keep busy.

When she arrived on the property, she saw a truck in the front. Not Adam's, but that would be a good thing; she could see some of the staff on site.

A man wearing a dark shirt walked toward her. As the figure came closer, she recognized Robert Parker. It took all her years of training and restraint to keep her smile on her face.

"I didn't know you were coming," he said with a smile in return. "Want to do a walk around with me?"

How many polite ways were there to say no? She'd come here to get her bearings. While thrilled Adam had asked her to help him out, she wanted to make sure she knew what she was doing, and she wanted some time to evaluate what was needed. However, no matter how many times she tossed the word around in her head, she couldn't come up with a way to say no to the person with whom she was partnering up.

Not that she was really paying attention, but she wondered how he got dressed in the morning. He had on a blue jean shirt with a black undershirt and jeans. It wasn't what he wore, though; it was that it all looked coordinated and neat.

"I can come back later," she said, "if you need time to do your assessment."

He grinned. "Are you asking me if you are going to be too much of a distraction for me to do my assessment? While I can see how that might be a problem, I think I'll be able to make it. Let's start with the grounds around the house."

Her mouth fell open. Not that he saw,

because he had already walked away. There were words for men like him: arrogant beyond anything. And what did he mean that she would be a distraction? Did he think she was attractive? It didn't matter what he thought, because she could tell he was just full of himself.

Robert was a piece of work that Delilah didn't really have an answer for. Maybe it was a good thing they had met here. She could help him stay focused and let him know how things would work. She wasn't going to mix business and pleasure. He needed to know that his comments like her being a distraction would not be going to her head. While nice to hear, his compliments didn't mean a thing. They just meant Robert was talented and had the gift of the gab.

He looked over his shoulder and waited for her to follow.

"Don't look so doubtful, Ms. Cade. I assure you that I can multi-task. Are you worried that I might fail?"

"Your flattery is not very convincing." She caught up with him, and they started to walk.

"Beautiful day, isn't it?" he said.

Delilah snorted. "It's the same as always. What exactly are we looking at?"

"Ah, all business. Perhaps I started us off on the wrong foot."

"There isn't a wrong foot; we are business partners."

"We need to be able to trust and be honest with each other. Right?"

Delilah rolled her eyes but kept walking. This was a trap. She'd known this man would be a problem from the first time she'd met him. As they walked along, the pond in the back of the site came into view and the ridge of trees that led to the forest in the back.

"Aha. I'm getting the silent treatment."

"In truth, Mr. Parker, you are getting the most polite treatment I can think of."

"I'm wounded and sorry I've pushed you to such lengths."

"Really? It surely doesn't seem that way."

He reached out and gently tapped her on the shoulder. "Forgive me if I seem forward. I didn't want there to be any pretense between us. I think you're a beautiful woman. We'll be working together, and I respect you for coming out here and helping your family."

Delilah gave his words some thought and nodded. "I admit I might have been a bit touchy. Thank you for the compliment, and as long as we keep our relationship professional, we'll get along just fine."

"So, we're friends again?"

Delilah smiled. "We're friends."

"Good."

"I'm doing this to help my family," Delilah said. "Is this a normal job for you or——?"

"I'm doing it to help the swamp men. They remind me of my old unit."

"Yes, I had heard you were in service. Sweet Blooms must be a big adjustment for you."

"I've been here for three years. It's different than what I had, but it's a welcome change."

Delilah found herself at a loss. She had just finished drawing boundaries on how things had to be, and now she wanted to cross her line and find out about his personal life. He *was* attractive. Wait. Was he really attractive? Had she really taken note of his handsomeness?

Robert Parker wasn't beautiful. His presence, though, caused her to take notice. It had been a while since she'd had any prolonged time with a man, but she'd manage it.

"How long have you been doing projects?"

"About two years," Delilah said. "I also do some consulting work on the side for friends."

He turned toward her as they walked along the river. "Quid pro quo?"

Delilah nodded.

"How long have you been in Sweet Blooms? I've been here for about three years, and I can't say that I've seen you as a regular."

Delilah smiled. "I've been visiting on and off to see my grandson. I finally decided to go back, and then the whole thing with Pierce happened, so here I am." She glanced around and noticed they had walked past all of the buildings. "Did we go too far?"

Robert shook his head. "I wanted to start from here. I thought it would be easier for me to show you."

Delilah nodded.

"The path starts here from the forest line and then we'll make a trail to go to the houses.

I think this will work for the swamp men and also give a second way to enter into the workshop."

Delilah looked around. She didn't really agree, but if he thought it was the best way to go, she'd run with it.

Robert stopped, and Delilah waited for him to give her some feedback on what else he wanted to show her.

"Yes?" she asked.

"Delilah, what's wrong?"

"Wrong?"

"Yes. I could tell when I was talking that you didn't agree with what I said."

Delilah thought about denying the statement, but then she just shrugged.

"I'm here to ensure what is done isn't something my grandson would disagree with and doesn't in some way go against our moral standings."

Robert shook his head and held his hands up front. "Whoa, Delilah. Let's get something straight. We are working together. That means we have to be able to talk to each other. We need to be honest with one another."

It had been a long time since anyone had really asked Delilah's opinion. While she'd had a wonderful marriage, her opinions hadn't been sought after or wanted.

"Okay?" she said unsurely.

"What's the problem with the trail?"

"Well, is the workshop for men and women?"

"Yes."

"This road seems dark. If people are coming on this trail, we would have to make sure there's good lighting. I'm okay here now, but tonight, it will be more intimidating. It's a safety issue."

Robert looked along the trail and then nodded. "You're right. One of the swamp men, named Tom, and his wife are expecting. Now that you've brought up the issue, I can see how she might not be comfortable here. Thanks for that outlook."

As they continued their walk, Delilah listened to the rest of what Robert said. She took notes and gave her opinion on occasion, but she was still in awe over the fact that he'd actually listened to what she had to say and wasn't just humoring her. Robert Parker was going to be more complicated than she'd originally thought.

———

Peaches wasn't as senior as Delilah had thought. The dog woke up at five in the morning. If Delilah didn't get up, then Peaches would start a low howl until she got out of bed.

During the past couple of days, Delilah had gotten more cardio than she ever had at any gym. Now she almost had her morning routine set up. She would wake up at four thirty a.m. and then take her rollers out of her hair. No alarm needed. The night before, Delilah always laid out an outfit, usually a sweatsuit she could don in ten minutes. By the time she finished getting dressed and doing her morning ritual, it was five a.m. and time to walk Peaches.

The pit bull wasn't a quick walker. In the beginning, Delilah tried to keep her on the busy neighborhood streets, but Peaches had a mind of her own, and they wound up on the quieter paths. As they both settled into a routine, Delilah used that quiet time to plan for the day. Today, however, she wasn't able to find inner peace. The problem wasn't the walk; she could pin the trouble all on one person: Robert.

She thought about their meeting yesterday.

She was still in awe over the fact he had asked for her opinion and really wanted it. She couldn't remember the last time her opinion had been asked for or valued. It had made her quiet and disturbed her in a way she hadn't been able to shake.

Even more impactful, she had to deal with Robert on a daily basis, and she wasn't sure what to expect. Robert didn't just remind her that she could add value to the project besides just monitoring; he also made her aware she was a woman.

If she was going to make it through to the completion of the project, she needed to find a way to make her interaction with Robert work. As Peaches pulled Delilah along, her thoughts spiraled into a vortex of indecision. How did women do this man-woman thing today?

As if the universe heard her and wanted a laugh, she glanced up to see the man in question jogging toward her. He wore a grey sweatsuit with a white line running down the outer pants leg. He didn't look winded, and he had a good pace. As he went by he waved, she saw young and old people turn to watch. Delilah found herself watching him as well.

He took long, sure strides and exuded confidence and success with every step. As he came closer, she saw some kind of phone strapped to his arm. Delilah would have turned at the corner, nodded and gone on her way, but Peaches had other ideas. When the dog saw him, she was revitalized and decided to go and greet him.

Delilah straightened her spine and tried to put on her most serene expression. When she and Robert met in the middle of the block, he stopped and jogged in place for a moment before tapping the device on his forearm. Then he pulled what looked like an earbud from his right ear.

Delilah pulled tighter on the dog's leash, because Peaches had decided Robert was the best person ever. The dog had sat down on the ground and was wagging her stubby tail incessantly and waiting for some attention. Seeing that she wasn't going to be moving anytime soon, Delilah fell back on what she knew: manners.

"Good morning, Robert. I didn't know you jogged."

His brown eyes held her gaze. "I didn't think you were interested either way."

Delilah counted to five in her mind. "I didn't mean to be churlish at the woodworking house," she muttered. "I was trying to be professional."

"We live in Sweet Blooms. We're neighbors who are helping one another."

Delilah felt like the fly that had somehow landed in the spider's web.

"Okay. I should let you go then, so you can finish jogging."

"I've done my hour already. This lap is my cool down."

"Lucky me," she said under her breath.

Robert bent down and patted Peaches. Delilah didn't see any stiffness at all in the dog today. The pit bull rolled over, bared her belly and nudged herself closer to get Robert to rub her a little longer.

A corner of his mouth turned up as he petted her. "What a good girl you are. How long have you had her?"

"I'm fostering her."

Robert looked up at Delilah and grinned. "She's an older dog. That's really nice of you."

Delilah acknowledged the praise with a nod, but inside, she experienced an inexplicable jolt of happiness. Robert gave Peaches one more pat and then stood up.

"You are pretty amazing, Delilah Cade."

She smiled and looked around them. No one else had stopped to talk to them or seemed to be looking. While it shouldn't matter, she was still the Cade widow.

"I'm not sure what the compliment is for, but thank you," she said.

"You help your family out. You foster senior dogs that are hard to get adopted, and you're smart. That makes you pretty amazing, and all in one attractive package."

"Thanks."

She hoped she wasn't blushing. She couldn't be sure if the heat she felt was the morning sun or the bevy of compliments resting on her cheeks.

"I won't keep you. I have to finish walking Peaches and get her to her grooming appointment." She was rambling. Delilah couldn't stop, because rambling was her first reaction to being nervous.

He didn't try to keep her. He nodded, said he understood and then told her he'd see her later.

"I can't wait to see what I found out about you next time we meet," Robert said before he jogged away.

She resumed walking Peaches, and her thoughts wandered. How could she work with him on the project if she couldn't even have a simple conversation without blushing?

Chapter Three

Robert already knew what he wanted to say to the room full of council members. He'd never been a great salesman. Whenever he needed someone to go along with a plan, he presented a proposal based on facts. As he looked at the residing council members, he didn't think today's meeting would be any different. The business would benefit Sweet Blooms and the swamp men. They would be represented as one unit, and he wanted some town concessions when it came to them having minimum orders.

Adam Cade, the well-to-do local boy who had returned home, had told Robert he had his full support. Adam had said Mayor Tamara Mason was a sensible woman and knew his grandmother. Mayor Mason was also very interested in any idea that generated revenue of the right kind. Despite Adam's encouraging words, Robert had made sure he was prepared with facts and figures. He understood he wasn't a known entity. He didn't hang out in the town at all. While he was respected, he wouldn't be the first person called on for a favor. Recently, he had witnessed how townsfolk had reacted to a vet. Caleb Mathews, who worked in the general store with Skye O'Malley, had told him people had assumed he had medical issues and then marked him as dangerous because of his military service. Not all people were that narrow-minded; Robert just needed to make sure none of them were on the council.

He didn't come in with a computer or any high-tech equipment. Instead, he provided copies of his plan as a ten-page handout. The council was smaller today. Hannah, Adam Cade's fiancée, had told Robert she wouldn't be at today's meeting because it would be a conflict of interest.

Robert's proposal was the only item on the agenda. The mayor had pulled him aside and told him that during the fair week, the council was reduced to three members and only pressing items were dealt with. Since Robert's plan had to do with the "supplies and gifts" in demand during fair week, it had been given precedence.

His thoughts wandered to Delilah, as they often did. What would she say about the gathered members of the council? He knew she was a woman of good character from the way everyone spoke about her. He wasn't blind and was glad her personality seemed as pleasant as her appearance. However, he was pleasantly shocked to discover the depths of her kindness and intelligence. Her compassion for people had made her think of the women coming to the woodworking site, and her compassion for animals had her taking care of Peaches. He had two dogs of his own, and he knew the demand senior dogs could put on a person.

Delilah Cade was brave and loyal: a golden woman. If the shoe were on the other foot, he doubted he'd have been able to be civil or keep a smile on his face like she had. She possessed all the qualities he'd want in a partner. Delilah was a golden opportunity he had to catch.

Mayor Mason cleared her throat, and everyone turned to her.

"Hello, Mr. Parker. We made the exception of hearing from you today because we felt the proposal you'd present would impact our current fair week. As a result, the essential council is here: myself, Clarissa Hastings, and Jerry Linden. Please start your presentation."

"Good morning." Robert opened the book in front of him. "If you'll follow along in the books provided, you'll see what I'm proposing, why, and how that will affect everyone going forward."

He waited until the council members had opened the plan and then began to talk about Nature Crafts, the group he and the swamp men were forming. He showed pictures of the goods the men made. He provided charts on what they sold for and how much they benefitted Sweet Blooms and the men. He outlined the opportunity for greater profits if the town requested goods on a steady basis. The men didn't have a problem producing the crafts if they knew their goods would be bought. They always fell short in supplying the town because they were never sure of the demand.

After about thirty minutes, he finished up

with the men being an asset to the town. They didn't live in Sweet Blooms, but they all paid local taxes. Robert also mentioned the support they had from Adam Cade.

"You've done your homework," Mayor Mason said. "For as long as I have lived in Sweet Blooms, the men have provided goods to the local stores. We haven't done a good job reaching out to them and seeing to their needs because we just didn't know how. Thank you for recognizing our deficiency and reaching out to them. Several businesses would be able to participate in this plan, so we should have some good news for you shortly."

"Thank you."

"With all of these plans," Jerry interjected, "do you intend to settle down here? I know you came back from the military, but you haven't had much interaction with the town save for your job in Skye's store."

Clarissa nodded. "Ah, yes. That's where I remember you from. You're the guard all the kids are scared of," she said with a smile that reminded Robert of a grinning shark.

"I'm not leaving the town. I'm committed to this venture, and I'm doing some work with Delilah Cade on her grandson's woodworking project."

Clarissa leaned forward, letting her chest rest on the table and bringing attention to the straining buttons across her bosom. If she took a deep breath, the pink shirt would pop open.

"It seems you have a relationship with the Cades," Clarissa said.

"Really, Clarissa. Again?" Mayor Mason chided.

Clarissa gave her a look over her shoulder but pressed on.

"If the Cades made a donation to the city,

it would be appreciated. It would show you are very focused on helping Sweet Blooms."

"Enough!" The mayor frowned. "We as a council are not a pay-for-play despite how the individual members on this board may function."

Clarissa sat back as if she had been rapped on the knuckles. "It was just a suggestion."

The women were at odds, and this wasn't an old argument.

"In regards to my relationship with the Cades, it's my understanding that Adam wants to help the town long-term and has decided the woodworking school and classes would do that. Other than that, you'd have to petition him directly."

———————

Some things never change.

Robert got into his truck and drove away from the council. They'd spoken about money and the Cades, but they'd barely paid any attention to the swamp men and their plight. He should have been used to being ignored but expected to work. In the military, people didn't think about the toll the work they did had on them or on the family of guys in his unit. His team had been a tool and could have been sent anywhere to do anything. The swamp men didn't fit in with "polite" society. They were old-fashioned, gruff, or didn't have the right look and made other people uncomfortable.

He'd found a way to make a living despite how people ignored him. The swamp men hadn't. They existed on the edge of town, and when people needed them and their goods, they were remembered. What about the swamp men's needs the rest of the year? Robert thought about Tom and his wife. They would soon have another mouth to feed.

Robert hadn't been thinking about his destination, but ten minutes later, he wound up at the Cade ranch. Delilah would be there going over the new building's specs. He had already seen them and thought to give her some time to process things. After the council meeting, he needed to see her.

At the ranch, he was given directions to the temporary structure built on the property. He was going to use the shed as temporary storage. When he heard Delilah was there, he was curious about the turn of events.

Robert went into the structure, but stayed in the background so as not to disturb the group that had gathered within. The walls were plastered with plans showing how the woodworking house would be built and how the surrounding property would look.

Delilah was holding court. She stood in the middle of the room while the architect and the foreman took notes.

The men listened diligently, and so did Robert. She laid out the building and asked for some amendments. While the structure accommodated the men and had a state-of-the-art air filtration system, Robert noted she had enlarged the windows to look like bay windows, to allow more natural light inside.

He looked at the postures of the men, and they were attentive to her suggestions. When she spoke, they questioned why she wanted a change or wished to remove the original structure. She added wide open spaces and a small kitchen as opposed to the large lunch room.

Once she was done with the physical structure, she addressed the colors and the furniture she wanted, as well as the landscaping.

As the session wound down, the architect got fidgety.

"Mrs. Cade, before I redraw all of these plans and redo the budgets, I'm going to need the approval of the project manager. He may not agree we need all of these on the first run."

Delilah smiled politely and became more reserved as she nodded. She wilted a little and mumbled, "Of course."

Robert didn't even think to stop himself. "Mrs. Cade has complete freedom and authority to make changes. She's here to give her professional advice and guidance on this project. I'm sure whatever she suggests, I'll be okay with."

When she looked at him, she had a smile on her face, and she stood a little taller.

The architect gave a curt nod. "Of course. We can meet after I've finished the new drafts." With that, he left.

Robert watched him go. That left the foreman. When Robert looked at the foreman again, he did a double take. The guy looked familiar.

He had dark skin and black hair with a natural curl. He appeared to be of Indian descent and must have noticed Robert's confusion.

"You must be Robert Parker." He held out his hand. "I'm Vihaan Linden, the foreman on this project and Jerry and Geeta's son. Nice to formally meet you."

"Same here."

They shook hands.

Vihaan appeared to be in his late twenties and about five-foot-eleven. He seemed competent and approachable.

"I heard you had a meeting with the council," Vihaan said.

"I did. I'm hoping we can agree on a business

proposal that includes the swamp men."

"It's good that someone is looking after them. My mother takes them food whenever we hear about a brush fire in the swamp. It can be devastating for them."

"I've had some meetings with them, and that's come up a time or two. It was one of the reasons I thought establishing a group with steady income would give them some security."

Vihaan nodded. "I hear they don't trust easily, so you must be a patient man."

"When I set my mind to something, I don't stop until I get to the goal."

"Then we'll get along great. I don't like to leave any project undone or leave a client unsatisfied. I'm okay with the revisions as long as they happen before the build." With that, he gathered his documents and said goodbye to Delilah.

———

Delilah found herself grateful and anxious at the same time. When she'd arrived earlier, the architect had asked for the project manager. She had told him the project manager knew she was on site. At the time, she'd thought it enough, but when she'd suggested more changes and the architect had realized new plans were required, he'd become more resistant. When he'd objected, she'd held her tongue and tried to think of the best time to contact Robert. Then she'd heard his voice, and he'd said she had the authority to make the decisions like he could. She could've jumped out of her skin. She was still doing the happy dance internally.

Today he'd spoken with the town council. She was more than willing to put her victory on the side to address why he didn't seem as ecstatic as she'd thought he would be.

"Hey, thanks for standing up for me."

Robert shook his head. "The architect should have known better."

Delilah didn't know what had happened at the council meeting, but it hadn't been the easy pitch they had all assumed it would be. She thought about going to the Banter House, but it was a bit out of the way. She had already made biscuits this morning for Adam and the crew. There were still some left. She just needed to work up the courage to ask Robert.

Inviting a man to eat food she had made.… Her old-fashioned rules reared their heads. Was cooking for a man even a thing anymore? She took a deep breath and decided to put aside the questions of her worthiness and did she know how to entertain a man until she'd found someone to bounce them off of. Right now, Robert didn't look like he was in a good place.

"At any rate, thanks," she said. "You don't look as thrilled as I thought you would.

The kitchen is set up; we can have some leftover biscuits and coffee." She didn't know how appealing that sounded to him, but she hoped he'd accept.

He nodded, and with a burst of butterflies in her stomach, she led the way out of the temporary building to the kitchen. He was quiet the whole way, which told Delilah something was really bothering him.

In the kitchen, she set up two cups and pulled out some biscuits, honey jam, and soft butter in case he wanted it. After a couple of sips of coffee, she asked: "Where are your thoughts?"

"I'm disappointed in how people focus on the wrong things. It's one of the reasons I came back to Sweet Blooms. I wanted to be left alone, and I wanted to find something useful on a day to day basis."

After getting him a butter knife and opening

up the butter and jam so he could get either, she sat down and wrapped her hands around her coffee.

"You don't think the council will approve your request?"

"No, that's not it. I think they'll approve it. I'm not sure if they are approving it for the right reasons."

"Did you tell them it would bring in a steady income?" Delilah asked.

"I did. The Mayor and Jerry were interested in that, but they didn't seem to care about the swamp men."

Delilah sighed. "You want a lot, Robert."

"Do I? It's one of the reasons I came back to this town. I figured if the guild were going to happen at all, it would be more likely that people would be caring for each other. I thought when I came home, things would be different."

Delilah reached out and buttered a biscuit for him. "I have to say, you've surprised me. I might have been one of those people who thought that, as a single man who's also prior military, you didn't give a lot of thought to others."

"I've had my good and bad days. I'd like to think that I did what was best for others more times than not. I need the council, but I don't want to play their games."

"Then don't bother."

Robert took the biscuit she offered. "Thank you. I think the recommended path might be to play along until we get our buildings up and the contracts signed."

"The end goal is to do right by the swamp men and get Natural Crafters off the ground. Maybe you can have one or two 'poster guys' who wouldn't mind coming to town and being the faces of the group. If the townsfolk don't see any of the people, they can't acknowledge them."

He took a bite out of the biscuit and didn't say a word. She was hooked watching his fingers as he held the biscuit. After a moment, the silence got to Delilah. Was there a problem with the biscuit, or was he trying to find a way to tell her having a face for the swamp men was a naïve idea?

"You know what they say," she told him. "How you start is how you'll end. If you say the project is about the people, but you don't present anyone for them to see, and then you agree to whatever shenanigans the town council will have, then you are agreeing with whatever their point of view is as well. You have the advantage, because they don't know what to expect from you. You can do anything, and your current actions will fall into a range they have to accept as the norm."

Robert downed a couple more bites of his biscuit and then nodded. "You're right."

Shocked, Delilah held her coffee cup midway to her lips. "Really?"

"Yes. I've been so hung up on why people didn't have my initial point of view that I've been missing the opportunity to remake their thoughts through example. Thank you."

"I'm happy to be of assistance."

He grinned and took another bite. When did watching a man eating a biscuit become a sexy event? She looked away. She'd been alone for too long.

"I'm counting on your assistance throughout this project," he said.

She gripped her cup with both hands. If she hadn't done so, Robert would have seen her hands tremble.

"I think Evan would be the best person to represent the men." Again, Robert smiled at her.

She began to fidget and finally broke the silence. "Yes?"

"I keep thinking how you constantly amaze me. How have you been here in Sweet Blooms, but I never met you? I thought I had met all of the retirees."

Delilah chuckled. "I'm not considered a retiree. They just see me as the Cade widow."

"I see you as an intelligent woman named Delilah."

She stilled. When she looked up from the cup, she saw him watching her and waiting for a reaction. She wasn't ready to address his words. She wasn't sure what was between them, but whatever it was, and wherever it was going, she wasn't ready.

"Did you want something else to eat?"

"No, thank you. The biscuits were good, and the coffee hit the spot. I've got to go and take care of my dogs."

"I didn't know you had dogs."

"Another thing we have in common." Grinning, Robert stood. "I have two who are seniors."

"Peaches is a handful. I couldn't imagine caring for two Peaches."

"I have patience."

"A great characteristic." Delilah walked ahead of him to make sure he got to his truck. "This is you," she said.

"Until we meet again." Robert reached out and picked up her hand. On it, he placed a light kiss. If the tingly feeling Delilah experienced was any indication of what was to come, she'd better consult a woman who had been in the relationship game longer than she.

"Thank you for the biscuits and conversation." Robert got into his vehicle, and Delilah stood there and watched as he disappeared down the driveway.

Chapter Four

The following day, Delilah met with Hannah Jenkins. At least, she would be Hannah Jenkins until next year, when she would marry Adam and become Hannah Cade. Delilah decided to meet the young woman on the ranch. No sense in going into town. Besides, any conversation held in the Banter House could potentially be repeated before Delilah and Hannah had even left the booth.

When the young woman walked into the kitchen, Delilah saw a glow to her skin.

"Someone has been to Lucy's," Delilah commented.

Hannah smiled and ran her hand over her rosy cheeks. "The facial was a present from Adam. Nathan is away with his dad for the week before school starts. Adam thought it would be a good time for me to spoil myself."

"I agree."

Hannah got a cup of coffee and took a seat.

"I'm sure you didn't call me to compliment me on my spa treatment. How are you?"

"I'm good." Delilah needed to get to the point, and now that Hannah was here, she found it difficult to bring up the issue she wanted to discuss.

"Any problems with the project?"

Delilah got up and made herself a cup of tea. When she was nervous, she needed to keep her hands busy.

"The project is going fine. To be truthful, the only question I have is how to deal with my partner."

"Robert?"

"Yes, Robert," she said with a sigh.

"Is there a problem between you two?" Hannah asked.

Delilah cleared her throat and sat down at the table. "I don't think we have a problem. The issue is, I'm not sure how to handle a man in this modern age."

Hannah smiled. "I've talked to Robert. He spoke very highly of you. He considers you to be an asset; someone who is really adding to the project. He updated us about the situation with the architect." Hannah leaned a little closer. "He's very interested in you. Is that a problem for you?"

"Yes…. No!" Delilah blurted. "What I'm saying is, we are business partners now. It seems like he wants to be more than that, but I'm not sure I know what "business partners" means today."

"Are you interested in him? Do you want us to intervene?"

"No, I don't need any intervention. It's just—"

"Just?"

"I'm the Widow Cade, Hannah. I don't date, and I haven't been on a date for a while. When my husband passed, that was it for me. I wasn't interested in another relationship. I had children to raise and bills to pay. By the time I had settled my children, I had to make sure the business stayed afloat. Fortunately, Adam took an interest in it, and he was talented. As he grew older, I stepped out of the way. I'm happy to be able to help now, of course. So, as you can see, I wasn't expecting Robert."

"Aha." Hannah smiled. "What would you like to know?"

Delilah smiled. "I'm so glad you understand."

Hannah grinned. "Yes, I finally do. You like Robert."

Delilah shook her head. "I don't know if I like him. That seems like a big jump, all things considered. I think he's a handsome man. Anyone looking at him can tell that. I also think he's pleasant to be around."

Hannah laughed. "How handsome? Is he *take a look at but keep moving* kind of handsome, or is he *we need to really take a moment and appreciate him* kind of handsome?"

Delilah cleared her throat and sipped her tea. "I think it's safe to say I could be attracted to him."

Hannah looked at Delilah over the rim of her cup.

"The rules governing how men and women interact have changed. I don't want to make a fool of myself."

"Well, not that much has changed. If you like each other, tell each other and go from there," Hannah said.

Delilah nodded. "Then it's not a big issue at all. I was a little nervous. I mean, I watch television and listen to the radio. They talk about this foolishness where women are so liberated, they don't expect men to do anything anymore."

Hannah held out her hand. "Hold up. Some women are like that."

"Like what?"

"They want to do things for themselves," Hannah said.

"Of course, I completely agree with being independent. I don't need a man to tell me how to run a house or take care of the kids. My job is my job, and my personal time is my personal time."

Hannah looked skeptical. "Woman can do that, but they also work outside the home and, more importantly, are sexually liberated."

Delilah paused. "Sexually liberated? I was married for 20 years. I didn't know I was in sexual prison."

Hannah shifted in her chair. "I'm not saying you were, but if you wanted to have sex with someone, you could, and you wouldn't be judged. Or, if you wanted to live with someone, you could without judgment."

Delilah raised her eyebrows. "Is that really true? Do we know of anyone in Sweet Blooms who engages in that behavior?"

Hannah shook her head.

"I guess that means sex is still not talked about in public, men should be respectful of women, and folks keep a closer eye on the things a woman does rather than a man. Did I miss anything?"

Hannah shook her head.

Delilah smiled. "Well, dear, thank you very much. It seems like nothing has changed at all. I know exactly how to handle Mr. Parker."

———

Delilah was anxious for Robert to come out to the site. They had agreed to meet this morning, and she felt in a more stable place today. When Robert drove up to the front door to the new temporary shelter, she was ready. Her heart quickened as she took a breath.

"I see you've made some changes," Robert said.

"I'm a very visual person, and I didn't know what you intended for the other structure, so I had this one erected. I was actually surprised how easy it was to set up."

He looked around the shed. On the walls, she'd tacked up everything from color samples to new sketches.

"You didn't like the architect's electronic equipment?"

"No, I didn't. It took away all the history of what I was looking at. When we do it on paper, I can make sure we don't go over the same old ground again."

Robert grinned. "I'm sure that went over well."

"Funny you should say that. You would have thought the architect was going to have a heart attack."

Robert laughed and took off his jacket. "Walk me through, partner."

Delilah's smile widened. What a thrill, to hear him acknowledge her as his partner. She knew he meant it in the fullest sense of the word.

He followed her while she showed him how she had organized the project and how she kept track of progress. When she was done, she turned to him and said, "That's it."

He nodded. "I like the way you organized this. It's not the way I have mine, but it gives us two views on the same project. Having this type of data helps us to make sure we've covered all angles."

"Thank you," Delilah said.

"Thank you for?"

"People may ask for my opinion, but it's usually them being polite."

"I hope you know I take your feedback and opinions seriously," Robert said.

"I do, and I appreciate it," Delilah said.

"I don't suffer fools, and people generally find me to be too frank."

Delilah laughed. "I would have never guessed."

Robert joined in her laughter. "Okay, maybe you would have known that."

"It's no problem. I'd rather know where I stand."

Robert's smile widened. "Good. I'm frank, but fair. I don't say anything to be malicious, but if you feel I've done so, let me know asap."

Delilah was curious. "You're saying that due to past experiences?"

Robert sighed. "I'm not a young buck, Delilah. When it comes to the fairer sex, I'm not an easy person to be around."

"Not that I'm saying we're doing anything in a romantic relationship way, but if we were, you wouldn't have to worry. I'm not a quiet woman, just polite."

Robert laughed. "I'm good with that. In fact, I'm looking forward to it."

———————

"I'm sorry to call you over," Caleb Mathews said to Robert as he pulled into the driveway.

Robert shook his head and waited to hear what Caleb had to say. While Robert had been with Delilah, he had received a call from Caleb, asking him to stop by when he had the chance. That didn't bother Robert; he was on good terms with Caleb. What gave him pause was that Caleb couldn't tell him what the meeting was about. Caleb was still having an issue revealing the purpose of the meeting.

In Robert's experience, people had no problem telling good news. All of this stalling meant whatever would be said wasn't something Caleb wanted to do anyway. Robert thought he'd make it as easy as he could by breaking the ice.

"Did you get a chance to talk with Skye about placing some orders from the Natural Crafts guild?"

Caleb smiled gratefully, as if he understood what Robert was doing. "I did, and she's good with it. We always have a backorder, and Cassandra saw some samples during fair day that really impressed her."

Robert grinned. "She must be the lady with the beautiful lines."

"Excuse me?"

Robert sighed. "Let's walk?"

Caleb nodded. "We can take this trail; it loops around the house."

They were on the path for a moment before Robert decided to explain his comment.

"Evan mentioned he had met a woman who had beautiful lines. When you said that Cassandra went to get samples, it all made sense."

Caleb smiled. "She's a good woman and friend to Skye."

Robert kept walking, waiting for Caleb to speak. When he didn't, Robert said: "Evan is going to be the face of Natural Crafts. What do you think?"

Caleb nodded. "He's single, even-tempered. He's a bit absorbed with his work, but all in all, he's a good representative of the group."

They had made it back to the front of the house. Robert stepped in front of Caleb and stretched out his hands.

"Listen, you called me out here. What was on your mind?"

Caleb sighed. "I was nominated to find out your intentions toward Delilah."

Robert frowned, not sure he'd heard Caleb correctly. Seeing how uncomfortable he was, Robert had to assume he had heard the man right. Now he understood Caleb's behavior.

"I'm curious. Who wants to know my intentions, or am I not allowed to know?"

Caleb let out a deep sigh. "You're taking this way better than I thought you would. Let me explain."

Robert smiled and then gestured toward the steps. "I'd like to sit while I hear this one."

"Delilah had a conversation with Hannah," Caleb said. "Hannah and Skye are best friends. They both adore Delilah and wanted to make sure she was okay. They thought about asking Adam to talk to you, but they didn't want Delilah to be embarrassed."

Robert halted him. "How does Delilah get embarrassed?"

"Well, if Adam asks you, he'll ask Delilah if she's dating, and I'm told no grandson should ask his grandmother if she does that kind of thing."

Robert took in the red-faced Caleb. The man, prior military, had gone on more than his fair share of clandestine missions. Caleb had been in dangerous situations, and on some occasions had had to shoot his way home. Yet today, the man Robert would trust with his life in a fight was flustered over the request of two young women who were concerned for Delilah. Robert didn't know what was funnier: Caleb's position or that they thought to ask him his intentions.

Robert stood up and looked at Caleb. "So this is what love does to rational men?"

Nodding, Caleb grinned back. "It's true. I didn't even think of telling Skye no when she asked me to talk to you. I don't regret a moment of loving her."

Robert nodded. "Nice to know what I have to look forward to." He turned and walked toward his truck.

"You didn't say what I should tell them."

Robert looked over the truck door. "I want only the best for Delilah. I'm hoping she sees that's me."

Chapter Five

The townhouse Delilah had rented reminded Robert a lot of her. The building was set back a little from the road. If he hadn't known what he was looking for, he might've missed it. When he did find the driveway, it welcomed him with flowers along the side of the drive that led to a bright, light-blue house decorated with baskets of hanging flowers. A white picket fence surrounded the townhouse. Secured in the yard with a very long leash was Peaches.

He looked at the leash. *Cute.* It was so long that when he went to the fence, Peaches eagerly met him at the door. With a command, he stopped her from jumping, and she sat at his feet, waiting to know what he'd like to do. When she realized he wasn't there to play with her, she went back to her dog house.

A well-cut lawn that looked regularly tended fronted the townhouse. Also in front of the building were two seats and a white table underneath a pinstriped umbrella.

After talking with Caleb yesterday, and in lieu of their aggressive build schedule, Robert wanted to make sure they both understood his intentions. He'd called last night and apologized for phoning late. He'd asked if he could stop by before she took Peaches to her daily doggy daycare. He looked at the work she'd put into Peaches and wondered if Delilah knew she wasn't going to give the dog to anyone.

He walked toward the three steps that led to the door, then halted as Delilah came out of the house with a tray in hand.

"Oh, you're here! I'm just in time, then."

He stepped back while she set up the table. She invited him to take a seat, and she poured them both some lemonade. After he had taken his first sip, he smiled.

"What would have happened if I hadn't wanted lemonade?" he teased.

Delilah smiled back. "I would have had two lemonades and promptly gotten you a bottle of water."

A delicate flush bloomed across her face. She must have felt it because she tried to cover it up by waving her hand over her cheeks. "The sun is a little stronger than I thought."

"I think it's actually a little milder today," he parried.

She stopped fanning herself and then put on her polite smile—the one that said she really wanted to say something else, but was going to go the safe and appropriate way.

"What can I do for you, Robert?"

"I'm here to clear up what might be a misunderstanding between us."

She swallowed and then placed her hands in her lap. "What would be the nature of this misunderstanding?"

"Did I mention before you are a handsome woman, Delilah Cade?"

Looking confused, she nodded.

"Did I also mention that you not only have a fine head on your shoulders, but you also have something going on inside that attractive head on your shoulders?"

Her eyes widened, and the corners of her mouth inched up a bit. "You hadn't told me so, but I did get that from your interactions with me."

"Good. Then it should come as no surprise to you that I would like to have a relationship with you."

She grabbed her lemonade glass. "You are direct."

"I am." Robert's gaze locked with hers. "It can be off-putting to some. I want to make sure you're open to the idea before we go forward."

"Why does it sound like this isn't going to be a *let's discover each other* kind of relationship?"

He smiled. "It might be, but I'm too old to invest in something and not let you know what I'm offering."

She nodded. "Go on."

Generally, Robert had nerves of steel. He had been in several dangerous and life-threatening situations. But right now, he felt as though he had more to lose than all of those times put together. He wanted to say the right things, but also wondered if he should hold back on all that he knew to be true about himself.

"Robert? Please go on. I'm listening."

Her gentle tone of encouragement solidified his actions.

"I'm sorry. Like a rookie, I was getting cold feet, because this is important to me. I want to have a relationship with you, but I'm a hard man. I don't do flowers and romance. I can't tell you that I'm in touch with my feminine side, either. According to most women I've dated, I'm a throwback and a caveman. I believe in equality as long as you know I'm paying for everything. I realize it's a new world, and I might be able to adapt to some of it, but all in all, what you see is what you get: a grizzled veteran who's seen too much and wants a simpler life. I'm looking to share it with a handsome woman with a good head on her shoulders. I see that in you, so I'm willing to try if you are."

He stared at her, waiting to see how she'd

taken his words. She picked up her lemonade and took a sip.

"I see you've given a lot of thought to what you are offering."

"When you're alone, like I have been, you have time to think about what you'd like. You just don't know if it will show up," he replied.

"You've been candid, so let me be the same. I'm a widow. I've been with one man my whole life. I married him, I bore his children, and that has been my life. I've gone on dates, but I'm not into 'friends with benefits,' freebies, or discovering my new freedoms now that I'm past the age of sixty. I wish I knew what baggage I have, but I don't. If you really want to be with me, you have to be prepared to deal with my baggage when it comes up. We'll be in the same boat. If you think you can manage that, I think we can give this a try."

He picked up his lemonade and held it in the air, waiting for her to lift hers as well. "Let's toast to us giving it a try and finding out where we end up. To happy endings."

Delilah raised her glass. "To happy endings."

They both sipped. When he placed his glass back on the table, he let out a big sigh. "So, that was the first item I wanted to address."

Delilah cleared her throat. "There's more?"

Robert smiled. "There is. Now that you know I'd like to date you, let's address our business relationship. I keep my personal life separate from my business one. While we are working together, I think we should make sure the two relationships don't leak into one another. Agreed?"

Delilah smiled. "Agreed!"

Robert stood. Once he was on his feet, he bowed. "Thank you, and now that we've cleared that up, I'm good to go. I'll see you at work tomorrow morning."

———————

Sitting across from Delilah in the waiting room, Hannah smiled. "First a spa day, and now a mani-pedi day. This has been the best time I've ever had while Nathan is with his dad."

Delilah thought back to what Robert had said to her. She was ready to let the world know she was about to try dating again. Now that she had something solid and she had a person she was going to engage with, she wanted the younger woman's feedback.

"It's not a lucky break, Hannah. This is a bribe to get you to my side."

Hannah opened her eyes and reached out to touch Delilah's hand. "Luke, he is your father."

Both women laughed.

"I wanted you to be the first to know. I'm going to date Robert Parker," Delilah said.

"Is this one of those secrets like Vegas?" Hannah grinned. "What's said at the spa stays at the spa?"

"Actually, it's not. I just wanted to get your reaction first. It will help me prepare to tell Adam."

The younger woman leaned forward and patted Delilah's hand. "We are glad you and Robert have decided to date. We weren't clear about his intentions, but he's made them clear to you."

Delilah smiled. "Yes, he was very clear."

"I can see from your smile that whatever he said or did, he managed it with taste and style. You seem pleased, and that is all we wanted."

Delilah was glad Hannah was on her side. The whole situation with her and Robert made her nervous still. Last night, the doubts had set in. What was she doing dating? If she dated, did that mean she was disloyal to her husband's memory? Could she still call him her husband if she was thinking about entertaining another man? Was she ready to be intimate with a man at her age? Like a dam that had broken open, the doubts flooded her.

"Thank you for your support," Delilah answered.

"You said thank you, but I heard all that reservation in your voice. What's wrong, Delilah?"

"Is it that obvious?"

Hannah laughed. "I'm the queen of self-doubt, so it is to me. I would think you'd be ecstatic."

Closing her eyes, Delilah spoke from her heart. "I'm a little intimidated by him. He's all put together. He can itemize what he wants at any time, and I'm me."

Hannah nodded. "It may not make a lot of sense, but I'm relieved that he chose you. He saw something in you that, despite his personality, he thought would work with him. You need to trust that he knows what he wants, and he knows how to get it."

"Trust is a big word for me."

Hannah sat up. "Isn't it a big word for us all?"

Delilah paused. "I don't know. Years ago, when a woman said she trusted a man, it meant she put her life in his hands. To trust him meant to give him full access to her secrets; to know he would be there when she needed him, and that he was the last line of defense. That's what trust means to me."

Hannah nodded. "Trust means that to me, too. I don't just give it, though. It has to be earned. When we just give it, we don't put enough value on ourselves. When it has to be earned, it speaks to what our own self-image and self-worth are."

Delilah agreed. She didn't know if she could do that trusting thing in practice, but she agreed with what the younger woman had said. Hannah rubbed her hands to get her attention.

"The important thing is to remember you are the one in control at all times. If the relationship works, you can move forward. If it doesn't, you can break it off."

The receptionist from the spa walked into the room and announced they were ready for them. For the rest of the day, Delilah answered all of Hannah's questions, but she was distracted; her mind rolled around the ideas of trust and how she controlled the relationship.

The next day, Delilah went to the project site. If she was in control of her relationship with Robert, then she had no idea how to work the reins. She showed up on site and worked all day.

She went over plans. She and the architect sketched and resketched some of them until she thought she could draw the landscape herself. She became short with the architect who was already testy. When Vihaan came by, he suggested they go look at the landscaping itself because he needed to understand the budget and the vision.

She'd been outside discussing plants in such detail, she'd never look at another plant, bag of mulch, or ornamental bush the same way again. They had sniffed redwood chips, which smelled great but bred mosquitos. She had just finished feeling the texture difference between dark, rich dirt and dark dirt infused with clay. As she and Vihaan were trying to get the red off of their hands, Robert, carrying two water bottles and an umbrella, came around the corner.

What had he been doing all day? She was feeling insecure and not at her best. Delilah touched her hair and brushed off her clothing of non-existent lint. He, on the other hand, looked as handsome as ever. He wore a polo top that never got wrinkled or even entertained letting sweat stain it in any way. She could barely keep cool in the sundress she had on, while he looked like he traveled with air conditioners around him 24/7.

"Yes?" she snapped before she could get a hold on her frustration.

"I noticed you two were so engrossed in your work, you forgot it gets hot standing in the field."

He had brought the umbrella and water for her and Vihaan. "I didn't think I'd be out here this long. Otherwise, I would have brought water."

Robert smiled. "It was my pleasure to bring it. You were working so hard, you were making us guys doing the clean-up in the building feel like we were slacking."

Delilah tried to read him. The light banter wasn't her normal, and she wasn't always sure when the jokes started and stopped.

"I'm sure you were all doing good work," she said, hoping to smooth over any perceived hurts.

"Why don't you come inside and look at the progress we've made?" He motioned to the main building with his packages in hand.

She walked inside and saw the crew had removed all of the debris from the main room. They had taken out the barn's stalls as well. In the middle of the room were piles of construction material to be used for indoors. The building looked completely different from when she had seen it just a couple of days ago.

In the eating area, the crew had set up a temporary table. On it was the framework for the larger windows she had asked for. As she walked around, she forgot how miserable she had been outside.

"Please, have a seat." Robert gestured to a chair.

She sat. He went to a nearby cooler she hadn't noticed before and pulled out a plate of cheese and crackers. She raised an eyebrow. Next would he open up the mini buffet?

He pulled out long-stemmed plastic glasses. He then poured a white grape wine in them. She couldn't believe how he had taken away her discomfort and managed to resolve what she'd thought would be an uncomfortable moment with a calming snack.

"Anything else I can get for you?"

Delilah smiled. "No, I think you've thought of everything. Thank you."

She was about to reach for the glass when she saw her hands were still stained with clay, and she instinctively pulled them back. Maybe he hadn't noticed. She should have known better. He walked over to a cabinet and pulled out a box of wipes.

"The workers use them to remove grit and dirt before lunch. You know I already think you're amazing. I don't need you to be perfect," Robert said with a smile.

Delilah grabbed the box and wiped her hands. "You say that now."

Robert chuckled." Where would I be if you were perfect?"

Delilah wanted to say where he was now. She waited until he sat and then made a small plate of cheese for them both, even adding the toothpicks. After setting both plates up, he raised his glass.

"To new beginnings."

She nodded.

"I'm not trying to be perfect," she replied. "I make mistakes all the time."

"Really? Name the last time you made a mistake and didn't correct it," he teased.

She rolled her eyes. "There. I did it."

"What?" He sounded confused.

"I rolled my eyes. It's obviously a mistake, but you tend to push me toward some very unladylike moments."

Robert laughed. He reached across the table and placed his hand over hers. "You can be you with me, Delilah. I already know I want the woman beneath."

His words lulled her into a sense of security she hadn't felt since being with her husband. How did Robert seem so calm and easy when it came to dating? She had to control herself when he reached out to touch her.

She wasn't married anymore. It was okay to

have another man touch her hand. Robert was going slow for her, and she appreciated it, but inside, she worried. Could she do this type of interaction again, this thing where she would have to put herself out there again?

"Thank you," Delilah said as she pulled her hand back.

"You're skittish."

Delilah looked up and snapped: "Animals are skittish."

"I was trying to broach the subject delicately."

"Really?"

Robert sat back in his seat. "Do you want to start an argument, Delilah?"

"No!"

"Then talk to me. What am I doing wrong?"

"Wrong?" she echoed. Then she hung her head and sighed. "It's not you, Robert. This is all new to me. I may not be cut out to date again."

He leaned forward and tapped the space in front of her hand. She drew her hand back, and then he covered hers with his. "You are fine. We'll go at your pace. Remember, you're in control."

Delilah laughed. "It's funny; you are the second person to say that to me, but I don't feel like that's the case."

"Talk to me about your husband."

Delilah yanked her hand back and pulled it to her chest. "Excuse me?"

Robert sat back again. "You heard me. Talk to me about your husband. He's a part of your life and, by extension, our lives if we want to move forward."

Delilah blinked. The question had come from left field, and she was still trying to understand what he was looking for. "Gregory was a good husband."

"It's not a judgment, Delilah. Hearing about him is hearing about you."

She took a bite of cheese and then thought on it. "I met Gregory when I was young. He was a great guy. He would always make me some type of gift and leave it for me in a place I was sure to find it. It started small. Then, one day, he made me a snow globe. I mean, it wasn't really a snow globe; more like a circle within a circle, but it was beautiful. He wasn't that good in school, and by the time he had finished giving me all these gifts, I suggested we start selling them. He didn't want to go to college, so it all worked out."

"Sounds like you two were great partners," Robert said.

"We were." Delilah swallowed as memories flooded through her. "We did everything together. It was a shame that he took ill. We taught all of our children how to do woodworking and molding. That was how we made money, and it bound us together. As time went on, we found the kids had different talents when it came to cutting. He was a good man."

"Thank you for sharing with me."

She smiled. "Thanks for asking, but I have to ask why?"

Robert smiled. "I've never been married or had kids, but I do know that people come into our lives and we need to remember and respect them. I have had several team members come and go. One could never be better than another in the same position. I remembered and appreciated them all. I'm not trying to replace your husband. He has and always will have a special place in your heart. I'm just asking if I can get a little piece."

She smiled and studied their hands together, then looked up at him and nodded. "I think I can do that."

"Good, then we can start dating. I didn't want it to be me, you, and a memory dating."

"You're turning out to be not so bad of a person," she blurted.

Robert laughed. "I hope so. I don't want you to worry. Remember, you are in control, and you set the pace." He stood up and started to clear the table. Looking at the plate, she couldn't recall eating that much, but there was definitely less on the plate now than before.

She rose to help him and passed him the plate to dispose of. When she had passed everything, she turned to ask him what was next, but before she could, he pulled her into his arms. She didn't move. It was unexpected. It was odd. It was strange, and as the panic subsided, it was pleasant. He didn't push for anything more. It was just a hug.

"Do you want to try to relax a bit more?" he murmured into her hair.

"I thought I was doing great by not moving," she replied nervously.

"We're starting with low-hanging fruit, I see."

She leaned back and looked at him. "Low-hanging fruit? You're lucky I didn't reflexively hit you in the family jewels!"

He nodded. "That would have definitely changed the mood."

"Changed the mood—?" She shook her head as she laughed.

He looked at her for a bit, then tucked her layered hair behind her ear. Even that felt intensely personal to her.

"You're worth it, Delilah."

"I hear you, and you sound so confident. What happens if I don't live up to your expectations?"

Robert grinned. "How could you not live up to being you? Don't worry, this isn't going to be as bad as you think. Can we seal our deal with a kiss?"

"A kiss?" she parrotted.

"Yes, a kiss. It's a thing people do when they think they like each other. It can sometimes be a prelude to sex, but doesn't have to be. Sometimes a kiss is—"

"Stop! I know what a kiss is."

Taking a big breath, she lifted her face toward his. "Okay," she said cautiously.

He kissed her gently on each cheek.

She waited. When half a minute went by, she cleared her throat.

"Do you need water?" he asked.

"Is that it?"

"For today, yes, that's it."

She knew she looked confused.

"Remember, Delilah, I'm in this for the long haul. I have time for you to get comfortable with me. Now, we have a building to oversee and grounds to beautify."

Chapter Six

"Peaches!"

Delilah's voice came from outside the fence.

"Peaches, I don't want to play now, baby."

Robert walked toward the fence and peered into the yard. Delilah had on jeans and an attractive floral top with flowy sleeves. He could tell they were flowy by the way she waved her arms while trying to corner the dog and put a collar over Peaches' head. He would have thought she was dancing if he hadn't heard her exasperated tone.

Peaches' tongue was hanging out, and every time Delilah took a step, Peaches took two.

After two more times of missing Peaches, gone were the sweet, indulgent tones Delilah had started with.

She tapped the collar on her thigh. "Peaches, if you don't come here now, things will not go well for you. We don't have all day, and you need to go to the daycare."

Robert fought not to laugh. Delilah didn't realize that by tapping the collar on her leg, she was actually inciting Peaches to get ready to jump and run.

Delilah walked up to the dog, who waited until the last moment before she darted around her and ran to the other side. Robert pushed the door open and then stepped into the yard.

"Peaches. Here." He pointed to the ground. Peaches tucked her tongue back into her mouth and brought her wagging tail to sit in front of Robert.

He looked at Delilah, who rolled her eyes and put the collar on the pit bull.

"All things considered," he said, "I thought you'd be happy to see me."

Delilah grumbled. "Yes, yes, I'm glad to see you." She bent down and made sure the collar was secure before standing up and putting on a smile.

Robert laughed then.

"How long were you watching me?"

"Long enough to know you had no idea you were actually asking Peaches to play."

"I wasn't! I told her—"

"You told the dog?"

Delilah chuckled. "Okay. When you say it out loud—me talking to a dog—it does sound bad." The dog in question rolled onto her back and wagged her tail.

Delilah shook her head. "You'll get no belly rub from me!"

Undeterred, Peaches turned toward Robert. When neither party bent down to give her any attention, the pit bull sat up and looked at him.

"I take you in and feed you, and this is how you treat me," Delilah joked. When Robert laughed, she turned to him. "Thank you for your help. Without it, I might be running after her still. But what brings you by?"

"Ironically, I thought I would give you ride. I know today is your evaluation day for Peaches."

"Yup. I'm going to get her cleaned up and then evaluated for adoption."

She'd wilted on the last statement, but Robert didn't comment. He reached out.

"I wanted to be here for the both of you."

Delilah smiled. "Thank you. I didn't imagine this would be so hard, but I'm doing what's best for Peaches." Robert just nodded. He patted his leg, and Peaches got up obediently and followed him.

"You have a way with dogs."

"They are simple-minded like me, so we understand one another."

"Really?"

"It's true; a person should know his limits."

"We'll agree to disagree," Delilah said.

When they arrived at the testing center, Robert decided to stay with her. He could tell neither Delilah nor Peaches were happy to be there. The center had white walls, and on closer inspection, Robert saw it was another shelter. Peaches became more reserved. Delilah, worried about the dog, babied Peaches more.

By the time the assessor came to work with Peaches, Robert knew it wasn't going to go well. The assessor, a nice young man named Jay, explained he would take Peaches into a room where they could watch, and handlers would put the dog through a series of tests to see if she was at a point to be adoptable.

Delilah nodded, but Robert could see she was distressed. He guided her to the viewing room. Once there, they sat down and waited for the handlers to bring in Peaches.

"Do you think she'll be okay?" asked Delilah.

Robert nodded. "I'm not concerned about Peaches. Peaches will be Peaches. I want to make sure you're all right."

Delilah looked at him with wide eyes. She wrung her hands in her lap. "I'm worried."

Robert placed his hand over hers and gave her an encouraging smile.

"Listen, we're both here. We'll see where she is and then address whatever comes up."

Delilah nodded.

"No matter what, I'll be here. We'll go from there."

Just then, a guy walked in with Peaches on a leash.

"She doesn't look happy," Delilah murmured.

"Let's wait and see." Robert didn't want to agree with Delilah and cause her more worry. Peaches was definitely not as animated as she had been earlier. Gone was the happy dog that had been playing with Delilah that morning. Peaches' head hung low, and she ambled along.

The young man walked Peaches to a couch and patted the furnishing.

"Up!" he said firmly. Peaches looked at him and then the couch. When the young man repeated the command, the dog gave him another look and then sat down.

"Peaches doesn't like close cuddling," the assessor said in a loud voice.

Delilah covered her mouth. "He calls that cuddling? Just because she didn't like that couch, it doesn't mean anything."

The assessor retrieved a ball and a frisbee. He held them up in front of Peaches, and neither one of the items moved her from her space on the floor.

"Peaches isn't toy motivated."

Delilah harumphed next to Robert. He had to stop himself from laughing at her.

She pointed at the young man. "He calls those toys? She has her own toys, and she is a very toy-motivated dog!"

For the next forty minutes, they listened to the assessor criticize Peaches by saying she wasn't this or that. By the time the test was done, Robert was scared for the assessor. When the young man came out of the room, he seemed remorseful. Robert was holding Delilah's hand, and after listening to her, he knew she was mad.

"I'm sorry, Ms. Cade. Peaches doesn't seem—"

"Peaches is just fine." Delilah took the leash from the assessor. "Those tests made no sense at all."

The pit bull had perked up once back in the room with Delilah. When Delilah got the leash, the dog moved to her side.

"I don't know what those tests are supposed to show, but Peaches is a fine dog, and I don't think this environment was fair to her. I thank you for your time!"

The open-mouthed young man watched as Delilah left with a Peaches whose tail was wagging for the first time. Robert just smiled and caught up with both of them.

Once they were in the truck a stricken Delilah looked at him.

"What did I just do?"

Robert kissed her on her forehead, then looked into her eyes. "You did the right thing. Now, let's take Peaches to meet my boys."

———

Delilah tried to put yesterday's events behind her. She had been working with Vihaan and the architect most of the day. Well past lunch time, she finished with the architect. She had purchased a portable intercom, because it would be a better way to communicate. The monitor was in her portable shed. Delilah wanted to make sure it worked from the main house where the construction was going on. If she set up the intercom, then the architect could consult with the others. It was the best way to address the issue without complaining to Robert.

"Mrs. Cade, I can call you when Robert comes back," Vihaan said, peering at the time occasionally. "I'm sure he just got caught up, but he'll be back soon.

Delilah smiled patiently. "Vihaan, you don't have to stay. I'm going to finish up a project I started. I'm sure it will all work out."

Vihaan smiled. "Your spirits are always up. I have to say, it is very different dealing with you than it is my mother."

Delilah laughed then. "We all know Geeta speaks her mind. I'm going to check on something in the main house. When you are done, you can go." Vihaan nodded, and Delilah made her way to the main building.

It was a short walk, and she'd brought the other monitor. She'd turn it on in the main house and then move the architect tomorrow. Delilah liked Vihaan, but if she wanted to get through the project, she'd need some distance between herself and the architect.

Delilah entered the almost-cleared main house. The one or two remaining people were leaving for the day. She found the kitchen area and, remembering the impromptu cheese plate Robert had made, ran her hand over the top. She placed the monitor down and turned it on.

"What took you so long? And what's your problem?" she heard Vihaan ask.

"Really, you've got to wonder why we're here." Delilah cringed to hear the architect's voice. "Vihaan, think about it; we were here first, and we had done all the work before the old woman showed up."

Delilah closed her eyes and reached for the monitor, not sure if she could hear traitorous words coming from Vihaan's mouth.

"You need to be more respectful," Vihaan said. Delilah dropped her hand. She knew better than to listen to this conversation. Her mother had once told her people who eavesdropped on other conversations couldn't really be upset because they were in the wrong from the get-go. Still, Delilah pushed all of that good advice to the wayside and listened.

"They need to be more respectful of us and our talents," the architect said.

"Why stay if you feel that way? It's not like Mr. Cade has paid you less than any other architect. I don't really understand why you feel as you do."

Delilah pulled out a seat and glanced into the outer area to make sure no one was left. She sat down and waited.

"It's not about money or getting paid. It's about sending her at the last minute after all the work was done, and for what? So she can put her name on our hard work? What value does she offer?"

"You don't understand what she says. I appreciate her point of view, given as a woman and as someone who has been in similar buildings," Vihaan defended.

"Yes, she was in a building like this when we were kids! Things change. Why should we be burdened with her? It's time for a new person to lead. Tell me, what do you really think about the suggestions she's made?"

"She brings up things I wouldn't normally think about. I wouldn't have thought about the windows for light, for example."

"Because we know how to bring in lamps. The natural light thing in the kitchen? What are we, flowers?"

"I wouldn't have thought about the lit walkways."

"Because you see well and your vision isn't going."

"I wouldn't have knocked down some of the walls like she did. That does make the space larger."

Delilah waited for the architect's sarcastic rebuttal.

"Okay, I'll give her that one. But what are we batting, one out of three or four?"

"What do you think of the project manager, Robert?"

"I think he's cool. He's military. Organized."

"You don't have any problem with him being older?" Vihaan asked.

"Please. He's done things and been places. You can't compare them."

Delilah turned off the monitor and closed her eyes. That was the crux of it. She had devoted her life to her family, not to her. She'd worked with her husband, helping him build a business. When he was done, she'd spent the rest of her life helping her children and making sure they were on solid footing. When that was done, she had spent time watching her grandchildren and ensuring they had the benefit of a stable home and someone who would go to all of their ceremonies.

Now, none of that was worth anything. She left the ranch and went back to her townhouse. Peaches was waiting for her. Delilah managed to keep it together until after Peaches' walk.

Once back home, she got ready for bed. She just fell atop the covers. Moments later, Peaches was on the bed as well. She snuggled right next to Delilah.

She wrapped her arms around Peaches' block-shaped head. "I matter to you, right, Peaches?" she said in a low voice. The dog turned her head and licked Delilah's nose. She gave a short laugh and pulled her closer.

Her heart grew heavy, and tears filled her eyes. She had no reason to be strong or to keep up appearances. She let the tears trail down her cheeks and familiar laugh lines. She had to accept the fact she was alone and had no place to be—a fact she dealt with every night. Everything and everyone she had sacrificed for had moved on.

Delilah wasn't sure she knew how to do something for herself and not someone else. She wanted to contribute her opinions to the project, but maybe the architect was right. She had so little to offer that she wasn't even worth keeping around.

Chapter Seven

Robert did his best to stay in the main building. Delilah was in what the guys affectionately called the thinking house. The reworked plans from the architect came over from the thinking house. When the men went to lunch, Delilah did a walk-through of the property and the main house. Vihaan would come over with updates, and for the most part, the arrangement worked well. Robert had seen Delilah work, and it fascinated him to see her mind in action.

Their time together was null and void, and today, he decided to fix that. After getting to the door and hearing the stress in Delilah's voice, he wondered if meeting with her was a mistake. Instead of backing out of the building, though, he went in.

"I know we have two doors, but we will need double wide doors for certain shipments," Delilah explained.

"To do that, we would have to redo the whole side wall. We've already wired that wall!"

"I hear you, but that was one of the reasons I said we should wait until all of the plans were done before doing any walls. We were all in agreement for the middle of the building and the center beams and electricity. The walls weren't decided."

Glad the doors had air pressured closure, Robert shut the door and then kept to the shadows in the back. The architect hovered over Delilah. She, on the other hand, looked calm and serene sitting at the table. Robert was the only one who would see her foot tapping underneath the table.

"I already signed off on the side wall," the architect snapped.

"It's unfortunate you skipped procedure. I can guarantee it's my approval that needs to be on the documents, not yours," she replied with steel in her voice.

"Really, I—"

"Is there a problem?" Robert moved toward them. "I came to help out if I could."

The architect faced him, and the man's shoulders slumped as if in relief. "We need to talk about the plans."

Robert raised his eyebrow and then turned to Delilah. "When you're finished approving them, let me know, and I'll look them over."

The architect sputtered. "There were some plans that I had approved, and—"

"I'm sorry, did you say you had approved plans?" Robert stared at the young man.

"Y-yes. I drew them up originally."

"You did, but only so they could be vetted by professionals."

The architect stammered and then nodded. "I have some business to talk about with Mrs. Cade."

Robert hadn't given any thought to the possibility of this kind of pushback against Delilah from staff. Pushback didn't really exist in his world. If a contractor didn't like him or his ways, he just fired them. He could see now that he hadn't set this up correctly, and he must determine how long the architect's resistance to Delilah had been going on.

The young man left. She collected her bag and cleared up her notes.

"Delilah, I didn't know—"

She whipped around and held her hand up.

"I can't talk to you right now."

Robert was confused. "What's wrong?"

She pointed to the door. "What was that?"

He shook his head. "Nothing."

"I'll tell you what that was; that was you breaking your own rule."

"How so?"

"You said you'd treat me the same. Do you think running to my rescue was a help? I have to be able to deal with my own problems."

"He was out of line."

"You are right; he was. It was my place to fix the situation, not yours. I'm going for a walk."

"I thought—"

"That's part of the problem as well." As Delilah walked by, she put her finger on his lips. "Don't think for me, Robert. I like you, but I'm my own person."

———————

Delilah didn't have any friends in the town. They were all back at the community center. She called them every so often, but she missed having a friend in town to meet up with at the coffee house to discuss moments of drama.

Some women had lots of friends. They had them from high school; she'd moved away. They had friends from college; she'd never gone, since she'd been raising a family. There hadn't been time to do the "regular or normal" things in life. She'd lived the life she had been dealt. Delilah didn't regret being a mother, grandmother, and support staff when her husband had needed it. Those things had kept her so busy, though, that now she found herself wanting and alone.

She stopped in front of a Starbucks. She decided to indulge in something sweet, pretty, and tall. She got her drink and took a seat. She was looking out the window when the chair in front of her suddenly became occupied.

"Hello. How's it going?" Hannah asked.

Delilah smiled. She genuinely liked the young woman. Hannah reminded her of herself in some ways.

"It's going," she replied.

"Ouch! What happened?"

Delilah sighed and shook her head.

"I know it's odd statistically that I'm with Adam," Hannah said. "I will understand if you don't feel comfortable talking to me."

"No, no. That's not it. I have had a rough day."

"I've got a nonjudgmental ear if you need one, or I have a *you are right and they are all wrong* ear. Whichever you feel you need."

Delilah laughed. "I might need a bit of both."

"Talk to me."

"Well, let's keep this between us. Okay?"

Hannah's expression turned thoughtful. "I will keep it between us as long as you aren't hurt."

"My physical well-being is fine."

"Then okay, it's between us girls," the young woman replied.

"There is a challenging member on the team," Delilah began.

"Fire him—"

Delilah laughed. "Let me finish."

Smiling, Hannah nodded. "I jumped too early."

"I have a challenging team member. I'm trying to find a way to address the problem and not stop the project."

"Fire him!"

Delilah looked at Hannah.

The young woman shrugged. "I'll think of another answer. Continue."

"I tried to deal with the problem today, and

Robert intervened. He was trying to make it better, but now I think it's going to be worse than before."

"Well, Robert did say he liked you," Hannah offered.

"He also said he could keep business and our relationship separate. That was his rule."

Hannah smiled. "We all say things we think we can do when it comes to people we care about. When it actually comes time to deliver, I think we all fail."

"Then how is this going to work?"

Hannah patted Delilah on the hand. "Let me give you this piece of advice. Whatever you do, I think you and Robert should talk about it. If you don't, it'll snowball into who knows what. If it's something you want to save, communicate."

———

Delilah went back to the ranch. She spotted a couple of the guys leaving for the day. When she asked them why there were there, they said a meeting was held regarding work. Neither of them looked her in the face.

"You're here to talk to the last one?" one of the men asked.

So that's how her luck was running. "Is the architect still here?" Better she straighten him out about whatever he thought was going on between her and Robert.

The worker shrugged. "I wouldn't call him that. He's coming," the man said, pointing.

Delilah turned to see Robert striding down the path. When he realized it was her, his pace slowed. Delilah sensed she was being approached like some skittish animal. Anticipation and nervousness built as he neared.

Besides being an attractive man, he was a force of nature that affected everyone around him. She thought about how kind and considerate he could be. Unfortunately, he wasn't sensitive all the time.

"You came back," he said. "Did you forget something? Is there something I can do?"

"I had to take a walk and speak with a friend. We need to talk."

"You know I'm here for you."

Delilah agreed. "Are you here with the architect?"

"No, he's gone. He didn't return."

"Good. I wanted to discuss today."

Robert stood with his hands behind his back; he leaned his head forward. "You have my attention."

She paused, stepped up and tilted her head toward him. Her hands were shaking. He must have noticed how nervous she was.

Now that they had made some declarations to each other, nothing could be ignored.

They weren't children, and they didn't need to play coy games. They were going to kiss. She'd give him a chance to have a place in her heart, and that meant they'd have some hard conversations. She had to decide how this relationship would be different and maybe even better for her than her last one.

She was about to embark on a journey where she made a commitment to herself. This relationship wouldn't just be about what she could give; it would also involve what was being brought to the table for her. She wasn't sure what that entailed, but this time around, she'd work on getting a better deal for Delilah.

It all began right now. Right now, she had to put aside her fear, nervousness, or maybe anticipation and excitement, and move forward.

Robert cupped her face. "Hey, it's not that complicated."

Delilah looked at him and blinked. "Really?"

"Really. If you want to talk, let's talk. If you can explain your concerns to me, I can try to understand them." He held out his arm, and she placed her arm in his. They started to walk. Doing the mundane task of walking, she could focus her efforts on putting her thoughts together.

"Thank you. I was tied up in my thoughts."

"What's on your mind, Delilah?"

"I wanted to say to you that I was angry."

"Ahh. This afternoon had a bigger effect than I'd thought."

She glanced to the side to see if he was joking. When she saw his serious expression, she went on.

"Yes, I got upset about this afternoon."

"Why don't you tell me what the problem was?"

"I did tell you. I was angry."

"Angry because of what?"

"You shouldn't have interfered. The issue didn't involve you. It was between me and the architect."

Robert leaned his head close to hers as they walked. "You're right."

"No, don't interrupt me. This is hard enough to— What did you say?"

"I said you're right."

She stopped unhooking their arms and glared at him. "If you knew you were wrong, why did you intervene?"

Robert kept walking. Maybe he wasn't going to answer the question. "The problem was," he finally said, "I wasn't ready."

"Not ready for what?"

Robert sighed and squeezed her hand as he held it. "I'm a product of my age. I came in, I saw you were being attacked, and I reacted."

Delilah frowned. "You made the big announcement that we would be working with one another, but we wouldn't be having a personal relationship on site."

"I did," Robert agreed.

"As soon as that announcement was tested, you suddenly had a different tune."

"You're right."

Delilah stopped walking and looked at Robert. "It's not doing anything for me to hear you agree that I'm right."

He held out his hands. "I care about you. I believed you were in trouble. I only intended to address the problem. I acted first and thought much later, although I have to tell you, if you hadn't been upset, I wouldn't have thought about it at all. I would have waited until you came back in the morning and asked if you still wanted the guy to work here."

"I'm actually confused about what to say and how to act," Delilah said. "On the one hand, a little part of me is happy you came to my rescue.

On the other hand, I'm conflicted. If you can't keep your word, what are we doing here, and how can I trust what comes out of your mouth?"

"Okay, I can see your point, and I want to make things better."

"You can't make 'I don't trust you' better," she muttered.

He took her hand and brought it to his chest. "I screwed up, but I'm old. I'd like a do-over; a trial period, if you will."

"A trial period," she repeated.

"One week. You'll see what you can expect from me."

Delilah looked into his earnest face while he rubbed her hand.

"I'm too seasoned for pretty words, Robert."

"Then give me a pass for being set in my ways. Let me show you how I can change."

She pulled her hand back. "What did you have in mind?"

A grin spread across his face. "Give me seven days to show you what I already know: You are the woman for me."

Delilah's cheeks heated. This was one of the many times she wished she wore some kind of makeup to hide the blush. "Fine."

"Do you need me to get you home?"

"No, I drove, and I need the time alone."

He nodded and then went on his way. Delilah watched him walk away. The handsome, confident, self-assured man was about to go on a seven-day trial period to win her affection. What had she been thinking to agree to that deal?

As she started for her car, she figured out a way to explain it all to him tomorrow. His trial period wasn't going to work. She wasn't interested in it because she couldn't be the woman for him.

Chapter Eight

Robert sat in front of Delilah's house and waited for her to come back home from her morning walk with Peaches. She should return any minute. He'd watched them leave and then he'd jumped her fence to leave his surprise.

He'd gone by the florist that morning. He'd asked for the oldest roses that were going to make it or be sold in time. He'd bought the bouquets and then had spread the petals all over the front yard. He'd then put a post in the yard that said: "You deserve to walk on petals."

He'd thought about what she'd said yesterday, and she'd been right; he had to prove himself.

He was used to doing that. A few moments later, she came around the block. As if Peaches knew he was there, the dog tugged on the leash. Delilah did a corrective tug, and then Peaches calmed down. Delilah looked beautiful in her purple sweat suit. He could see where she had run her fingers through her hair, and her cheeks were flushed from her walk.

He wasn't blind; she was still in good shape, with womanly curves that didn't need to be flaunted but played peek-a-boo with her clothing as she walked. She didn't advertise her shape, because her comfort was more important than the flash.

Behind those gentle brown eyes and underneath those subtle curves was a woman strong enough to ask for what she wanted. He'd seen her gentle side with her kids in the neighborhood, and yesterday, she'd shown him she wouldn't be a silent partner.

She'd become even more attractive.

When she opened the door, he heard her gasp in surprise. She dropped Peaches' leash and walked into her yard. He went to the door of the yard and waited. Peaches, not missing a beat, ran to him for a pat on the head.

"Oh, my!" she said.

"I brought the petals, since you're the sunshine." He gestured to the ground.

She smiled. "I know this is a trial period, but isn't this a bit much?"

"When the stakes are high, nothing is too much."

"I'm liking you better already." She smiled. "This *is* a bit too much, really."

Robert shrugged. "Not a problem. The petals were going to be thrown away. I saved them so their life would have some purpose."

She looked at Peaches at his side and the petals on the ground. Delilah shook her head.

He could see her losing her courage. He hadn't thought the petals would be too much, but perhaps his direct approach wasn't the right way to go.

"I don't think I can do this, Robert," she whispered.

"You can't do being given flowers?"

She took several deep breaths. "No. I don't think I can do this whole *getting back into a relationship* thing." She wrapped her arms around her midriff. "One day I might be able to do it, but I don't think it will be with you."

Robert traced her ear. "Tell me why?"

"I think you are amazing—great, even—but I'm not sure I'm ready to commit to a person like you. You are everything a woman could want. I just don't know if I can be all that."

He patted Peaches' head. He had to make Delilah see he was just like everyone else. "I have to say, when you describe me,

I sound really impressive. It humbles me that you think so highly of me, but at the end of the day, I put my pants on like everyone else. But most importantly, I know I'm the man for you."

Delilah looked around. "If this is just the beginning, you are looking for a different woman than me."

"I know you, and you are totally worth the effort."

She shook her head. "Robert, I'm flattered, but this is more than I think I can handle."

Robert stepped closer and leaned his forehead on hers. "Give it a chance. Give us a chance. You might be surprised."

"Robert, I think—"

"Don't think. Let's just be."

In her eyes, he saw acceptance and hope. "If we go ahead with this, what will you do during the trial period?"

"I'll change your mind and show you the woman that I know and care about."

"And the work?"

Robert nodded. "We'll handle the work issues, just like modern couples do."

———

Delilah went into work with Robert, and by midday, all was well. The architect hadn't come to the site, but was calling in all of his questions about the suggestions she'd made. Just she and Vihaan were sitting in the thinking room when the phone went off again.

"Let it be anyone but the architect," Delilah muttered.

She reached out to pick up the phone. She didn't want to talk about doors in walls. She didn't want to talk about how windows were destroying the balance by the pillars. She was getting tired. Her body was heavy and she felt as if she was dragging herself. She'd spent most of her morning dealing with him, and her mind was turning to mush.

Vihaan's laughter brought her out of her reverie. The phone had quit ringing. She picked it up to see who had called. Sure enough, the architect. She looked at Vihaan.

"Remind me why I do this."

Vihaan chuckled. "It can't be for money, because you are already rich. It must be for honor. That is the only other thing that makes a person endure."

Delilah let the stress of the day roll away. It was almost time for her to go home. It was almost time for her to meet up with Robert. The anticipation gave her a tingle of excitement of what would or wouldn't happen.

He was proving to be a man of his word. Robert wanted to show her how stable he was.

When the phone rang, she was so distracted, she didn't bother to look at the number.

"Yes?"

"I called earlier. Didn't you see the call?"

Delilah recognized the architect's voice. "Did we forget to go over anything?"

"I thought we did, so I phoned, but as I'm reviewing it, I see we didn't. I know you think I'm crazy, but the rumor is our project manager is going on a hiatus and won't be back for a while," the young man said. "So, I'm trying to get it all done today."

Robert was leaving?

"What did you say?"

"I know. Shock to me as well," the architect said. "When I talked to some other people he's worked with, it seems he takes assignments in different places. He may be out of the military, but he's still traveling the world."

"Let me get back to you."

Delilah was too stunned to speak further, and she certainly couldn't call Robert and ask him about the rumor. If she called wouldn't that be needy and desperate? She had to wait until tonight.

How could he do his trial period if he would be leaving? When was he going to tell her he was leaving?

Her phone buzzed; probably the architect. When she looked at the screen, it was a text from Robert.

Confirming I have the pleasure of your company tonight?

Yes, I'll be there. We need to talk.

I'm happy you agreed, but no man wants to hear that we have to talk.

No woman wants to say it.

With that, she put her phone in her pocket and went on with the rest of the day. The phone buzzed several times, but she didn't look at it. She lived from one task to the other until the end of the day arrived.

She had agreed to meet Robert at his house. There'd been some back and forth about him picking her up. After today's news, she wanted to go in her own car, so she could leave when she liked. Delilah was numb making the drive to his home. When she reached the ranch and went up the driveway leading to the front of his house, she was still in shock. She didn't get out of the car right away. Instead, she just let it sink in this would probably be the last day she saw him. Or at least, it would be the last time she saw him for anything other than business, and there would no longer be any chance of a romantic relationship between them.

She'd tried hard to avoid this type of anxiety and pain. Should have known better, right? All the signs said he wasn't the settle-down kind of guy. He had been in the military, always on the move. She had to stop going over all of the signs she'd missed. She could do this. After taking a calming breath, she got out of her car. By the time she'd reached the top step to knock on the door, it had opened.

Looking casually sexy, Robert stood in the doorway. Her heartbeat quickened and a lump formed in her throat. He guided her into his living room and offered her a seat. Sitting, they were almost the same height. She needed all of the advantages she could get for this evening.

"We need to talk, Robert." Good. She'd sounded firm, calm, and collected. None of her erratic emotions were coming through.

"Let's eat first. I've made some dishes that won't really hold. I'm trying to impress you with my many skills."

Delilah hesitated. She should get straight to the issue; the waiting would be worse. But a small part of her wanted to hold on to the dream a little longer. Robert was the only guy since she'd become a widow to get close to being Mister Right.

She nodded. Just a little bit longer before I pull the plug on the dream.

Robert knew he had work to do, but didn't know why. It was never a good start when a woman said she wanted to talk. Delilah appeared resolute and almost serene in the inevitable end, but still the most beautiful woman to him. No matter what she thought was an insurmountable mountain, he'd find a way around it.

When he sat her down at the table, she smiled, but her eyes held a sadness that he was determined to move. He couldn't just jump into discussing her concern. He wanted her to be comfortable so he could find out the root problem worrying her.

He served them both Chicken Francese with rice. He'd lit candles on the table and had adjusted the lighting in the kitchen. He tried to engage her in conversation, but she only gave one-word answers. After a few moments, he could see by the way she pushed her food around that it wasn't going to be a conversation he could control.

"Anything wrong with the food?" he asked.

Her head popped up, and he saw the Delilah he knew. She was concerned she had offended him and wanted to reassure him. As soon as she began to reach across the table, she yanked her hand back.

"Nothing's wrong with the food, but we need to talk."

Robert put his fork down and leaned back. "Okay. If it can't wait, go ahead and tell me."

She put her fork down. "Tell you? Isn't there something you want to tell me?"

Robert shrugged. "No."

"Well, let me tell you. When I spoke with the architect earlier today, he mentioned you normally take projects outside of Sweet Blooms."

"I do." Delilah seemed upset by his answer. Why?

She picked up her napkin from her lap and laid it firmly on the table. "You told me all those sweet words, and for what? I don't want to be home alone while you go to work! I understand if you need to—"

"Delilah, let me—"

"No. Really. I understand if you need to travel. I just wish you would have said—"

Robert grabbed both of her hands in his. She fell silent.

"Delilah, I have traveled in the past. I won't when I have you."

Her gaze softened. Then she shook her head and tugged her hands back.

"What's wrong, Delilah?"

"Tell me, when was the last time you took a job out of town?"

"Last month."

She shook her head again and rose from the table. Robert shadowed her but didn't try to stop her.

"Delilah, what's the problem?"

"An old dog doesn't learn new tricks that quickly."

Robert smiled. "I should be offended being compared to an old dog, but—"

"You know what I mean. I can't expect you to just change. What happens if we get through this trial and then you want to go travel? You don't have anything holding you here. I mean, you have dogs, but I assume you have someone to watch them when you're out of town."

"Yes, I do."

"See? You're not ready for a stay-in-town relationship. I need one, because I've done the wait-at-home-for-the-man-to-come-home thing, and I don't want to do that again."

Robert followed her into the living room and picked up her sweater. Delilah saw it in his hands and waited.

"I'm not stopping you. I'm helping you with your sweater."

"So you agree with me?"

"No, I don't, but right now, you have it in your head that what you believe is true. You don't understand your own power as a woman. I'm not interested in being anywhere but with you. I'm hoping you want to make a commitment, but with the limited information you have, I can see how the situation must look to you."

She turned after her sweater was on. "You

see we won't work out?"

Robert smiled. "I see now why you were frustrated and antsy. I see you're only going to believe when you think I'm committed. I'm okay with that. Like I said, I need a trial period, and during this time, it'll become clear what my intentions are."

Delilah shook her head. "I appreciate you trying, but I think we should just cut our losses here."

Robert walked her to her car.

"I'm sorry I ruined dinner."

"You didn't ruin anything. I'm glad you told me what was bothering you."

Delilah turned on the ignition. "I'm glad I told you as well." She had a sad look in her eyes. "Friends should always be free to speak about their issues."

Robert chuckled. "I agree friends should speak freely to one another. It's important that we are friends. However, communication is the key to all long-lasting relationships. This bodes well for us."

Delilah sighed in exasperation and he smiled to himself. She was scared and looking for any reason for them not to be together. Other people might see this as a setback, but to him, it was a good sign. If she were at the point of being scared, she had real feelings and didn't want to be hurt.

Now he had to show her how it was going to be. He couldn't wait to start wooing her. "I'll see you tomorrow, Delilah."

Chapter Nine

A couple of days had passed since the dinner at Robert's home. Delilah had seen him every day since. He'd picked her up in the morning after she'd walked Peaches, and they'd gone to the site together. His manner hadn't changed, but there'd been no more petals. No more impromptu lunches. Their relationship was ending, but she hadn't expected it to end like this. Her melancholy turned to anger. What kind of man didn't address the issue between them at all?

If he had decided it was that easy to forget her and move on, then she would do the same.

She stayed inside, going over the advertisements and items they could have on display during the open house. Skye had referred her to Cassandra Olsen for help with advertising. Skye had said Cassandra was a master at it. Just as Delilah was packing up her items, she noticed she was the only one inside. Vihaan had been in the building, but maybe he'd stepped out?

He came in the door.

"Hi, Vihaan! I'm going to—" He had a strange look on his face. "Vihaan?"

"Mrs. Cade, I think you should come outside and see something."

"Are you all right?"

He smiled. "I'm fine. Still, I think you need to see something."

Delilah put down her pocket book and followed Vihaan outside. A large group of people had gathered by the pond. Maybe a baby animal was there. Baby animals always drew crowds. As if everyone noticed at once, the group turned and saw her.

She nodded as she walked. When she got halfway through the crowd, they stepped aside and made a path. Someone had built the frame for a trellis by the lake, and they had included a bench. A sign had been posted on the frame, but she needed to get closer to read it. As she moved nearer, she noticed everyone in the crowd was smiling at her. They were goofy smiles of happiness. With the day she'd had and the way her and Robert's relationship had gone south, she could really use some good news now.

When she reached the front of the crowd, she saw Robert in a work shirt and a dark pair of jeans, with his sleeves rolled up to his elbows. Patches of sawdust covered his clothes. He looked amazing. He also had the goofy smile. She read the sign.

I'M HOPING DELILAH CADE WILL HONOR ME AND WALK THROUGH HERE AS MY FIANCEE OR WIFE.

She had to read the sign twice before the words sank in. As she walked toward him, she gave the wooden trellis a wide berth. People in the crowd laughed. She plastered on a smile and kept going toward him. As she got closer, she saw a small, round metal table, accompanied by two chairs, behind him. To say that she was beyond flattered would have been an understatement. She was also overwhelmed because it was the sweetest gesture ever.

"I'm going to kill you," she muttered.

"Ah. There is the Delilah I know," he replied in the same low voice. Then he raised his hand to the crowd. "Thank you, everyone, for helping me out and giving me such a grand send-off on my journey. Now, if you would, please, I'd like to start wooing my future fiancée if she'll have me."

Delilah didn't turn around; she heard chuckles and feet shuffling away across the grass.

"Delilah?"

She pointed at the sign. "Are you insane?"

"No. I know the sign is small, but I was building the frame for the trellis and let's say it's been a while since I've actually built as opposed to directed. It felt good to work with my hands again."

Delilah was speechless. He talked as if what he had done was normal.

"I made us some tea." Robert guided her to the table and then brought out two thermoses. "I should say I brought tea for you and coffee for me."

"Robert, we have to address the insanity." She opened the thermoses and poured them both beverages in the cups on the table. She tried to make slow movements while thinking about every magazine article she had read about seniors and dementia. What a shame that Robert was going through this hard time.

He placed his hand atop of hers. When she looked up, he smiled at her.

"I'm not crazy, demented, or in any way not sound. I told you I was here to stay, and I'm completely for commitment. How's your day going?" She couldn't believe how quickly he'd changed subjects.

"I'm not sure how this day is going at all. I thought I understood men, but you are a different breed."

He picked up his cup and toasted her. "Thank you. I'd hate for you to think your fiancé was ordinary."

Delilah tried to hold back the words, but they burst forth like a tidal wave.

"You are crazy! What do you think will happen when this charade is over? It will be the most mortifying experience for us"

She stared into her tea. Her vision got blurry, and she did her best to hold back the tears.

"When this is over, one of two things will be true. You and I will be together, and I'll be the happiest man on earth, or you will have decided that I'm not the one for you, and I'll be the loneliest man on earth, knowing when my opportunity came for forever happiness, I fumbled it."

Delilah gave Robert a sad smile. "I appreciate your words, but I've never been that kind of woman."

"What kind of woman would that be?"

"The kind men give up things for. I was a wife, a mother, and a business partner. I've always given," she said quietly.

"That was then. For me, you are the woman

I'd give up traveling for. The woman I'd give up working for. The woman I'd give it all up for as long as we could be together."

————————

Delilah wanted to get up and run away from the table. The conversation wasn't going anywhere close to where she'd thought it would. While she wanted to believe Robert, she wasn't sure she could.

"I know what it's like to give up everything for a person. I don't want you to do that for me, Robert."

He chuckled. "You don't get to be on both sides of the relationship. You don't get to say what you're worth to me and then say what I can and can't give up for you. It doesn't work that way."

"What do you want, Robert?" Delilah asked.

Robert leaned forward and kissed her forehead. "A chance. Another chance to prove I'm right about us."

———

Robert had wanted to redo dinner, and she'd agreed, but at her place. Delilah trusted him to be enough of a gentleman to leave when asked.

"Red roses are not only beautiful, but part of a tradition men follow to show a lady how much he admires her strength and beauty." Robert put her single rose in a crystal vase he had brought along.

Delilah looked at the vase and then back at him. "Roses have thorns. I'm surprised you didn't take those off of the long stem."

Robert shook his head. "Some things are worth the risk. I assure you, it's more romantic to appreciate the rose in its natural state."

Tonight's dinner was the chance he had asked for. Really, though, what could he say or do that would change her mind about their relationship? She'd thought about that all day long. It had made concentrating at work a beast.

They hadn't even talked about the subject yet. Every time she thought they were about to segue into the topic, her stomach tightened.

Finally, dinner was over, and they sat on her couch to have coffee. He had brought over some fresh chocolate chip cookies, and she'd agreed to make something hot to enjoy with them. She'd thought coffee would be the perfect thing, but now she found herself holding on to her cup like a shield.

Realizing she would probably pass out from anxiety if she didn't do something, she put the cup down and broke off a piece of one of the cookies. The cookies were sinfully good.

They were soft, but not too sweet. She knew they were from Geeta. For the cookies to still be soft, Geeta had made them fresh just for them. Why had he bothered going through the extra effort when there was no point?

Delilah popped the rest of the cookie in her mouth. "How did you get Geeta to make the cookies?" she asked. "She usually only bakes them for the school children, and even then only at special times."

He sat back and looked at her. "You don't think this is a special time? I'm trying to convince you that you're the woman I've been waiting for all of my life."

She licked the chocolate off of her fingertips. "No."

He raised an eyebrow. "Only a no?"

"Is there anything else to say?"

"You are an amazing woman, and this proves it."

Delilah was confused. "What proves I'm amazing?"

He laughed. "The harder it is to convince you, the better we'll be together. No one or thing amazing is easy to gain."

Such optimism. She couldn't help but laugh. "You must have been an optimist as a child."

"Not really."

She stared at him; he appeared relaxed on her couch. "You're not going to change me. I'm flattered but—"

"No matter what you say, you won't convince me."

"What?"

"You're scared, Delilah. If we start there, then we can work on the obstacles."

She glared at him and shook her head. "I told you I was scared to give any relationship a chance."

Robert sat forward until their knees were touching. "I think you're afraid I won't find you worth the trouble."

Nope, that couldn't be it, because she had already gone to several therapists to help her develop her confidence and self-esteem. Delilah wanted to reply with a ready comeback, but he'd left her thinking. While she pondered the effectiveness of therapy, Robert broke into her thoughts.

"Kiss me."

Delilah looked at him as if he were crazy. She was excited and terrified at the same time. That was the only reason her pulse fluttered so erratically. "Really?"

"Really."

She folded her arms over her chest. "I'm not some schoolgirl who thinks sex makes things better. I'm also not interested in a Mr. Right Now session."

Robert laughed. "I'm not interested in being your Mr. Right Now either. I just want to be your Mr. Right. You are a sexy, attractive woman. I'd be lying if I didn't say one of the reasons I'd like you for a wife is that I want to know you in the closest way a man and woman can know each other."

This guy knew how to spin it.

"Be as brave as I know you can be, Delilah. Kiss me."

His words were a dare and a promise all wrapped up in one. It was better to give in so he'd know they weren't meant to be. It wasn't just the dare but it would also be a way to set him straight. She leaned closer to him, and she expected him to meet her halfway, but he sat still. When she neared, he still didn't move. Once again, she was a teenager about to give her first kiss to Jimmy from around the block.

She eyed Robert's lips, closed her eyes, and then went forward.

At first, it was like falling out of the sky. She was moving through space, not sure of the destination or where she would land, and then warm, strong hands cupped her face. She turned her cheek into one hand and placed a chaste kiss on his palm. She opened her eyes, thinking he would expect his kiss on the mouth now.

"Thank you," he said, his voice gentle and his gaze steady. "You never disappoint and always confirm you are the one I've been waiting for." Then he stood. Delilah followed him and stood as well.

"We didn't kiss," she said.

"That was more than enough."

Delilah was confused. "I thought—"

"You thought what, my love?" Robert smiled. "You believed I'd start with a kiss and then ask for the world? I'm too old to depend on just great sex." He stepped back and bowed. "I think I should be leaving now."

"You feel nothing?" she asked in a small voice.

He reached out and lifted her chin up so light hit her face. "Problem is, I feel too much. I don't want happiness for the moment. I want happiness for a lifetime."

Chapter Ten

"You've ensnared the local catch," Adam said. "I heard about the spectacle Robert made of himself. I wasn't sure you appreciated it."

Delilah moaned to herself. Why, when folks got older, did kids and grandkids feel the need to self-appoint themselves as guardians? "I wasn't looking for anyone, but I will say that he wasn't a bad catch from the bunch."

Adam grinned. "I'm taking that as a yes." At five foot eleven inches, he was the spitting image of his grandfather. From the moment Adam had been born, Delilah had known he was the reincarnation of her late husband.

"You make me sound so picky!" she replied.

"No. I'm grateful you are so careful about who you are with." Adam kissed her on her forehead. "It keeps the private investigator bills down." Delilah shook her head at his joke. At least, she hoped it was a joke.

Adam had gone to the city to finish transferring his business to his sister. Now, he wasn't even on the board; no longer officially a part of Cade Designs. Adam had come to Sweet Blooms as part of him trying to find a wife and settle down. Fortunately, he'd found Hannah, who was as close to him as Delilah knew two people could be.

Delilah endured the small talk about the project. How was it doing? How did she feel? Adam even asked if she was getting enough sleep. The more personal the question, the more uncomfortable her grandson became.

"I assume you're here for a reason other than

my health? As you mentioned, Robert made a spectacle of himself."

"All of the women who told me the story said he threw himself at your mercy." Adam grinned. "I would have liked to have seen it."

"Did they tell you he built a silly trellis on the property?" she asked.

"Yes. I heard he did it with his own hands. Robert doesn't really do building, so I'm properly impressed."

Delilah didn't know what she thought about Robert anymore. He was making her face herself, and that made her uncomfortable.

"Maybe we should talk about something else?"

Adam moved to stand in front of her. "You know, if you don't like him, I can get rid of him." He winked.

Delilah stared at her grandson and shook her head. "That time has come and gone, Adam.

Your generation fights on social media to get rid of a person."

Adam shrugged. "All joking aside, I want you to know that if you're not happy, that is what matters."

"This is a small town, and…."

Adam pulled Delilah into his arms. "I love you more than you know. No project is worth you being unhappy. No person is so important that I would put them above you. You have a special place in my and Hannah's life. You want to see Hannah's mama bear instincts come out? You are our only concern. Let me know: Do you want us to move Robert, or are you okay?"

Love had pushed Delilah into a corner. In this moment of truth, she had to ask herself the questions she was running from. Was Robert right for her? Was she just scared? Adam had offered her the perfect opportunity to go back to what she knew and what she had been doing for the last ten-plus years.

She let out a sigh. "No, he's okay. He's just unexpected."

Adam pulled back. "Unexpected in what way? Men have always looked at you." He wiggled his eyebrows. "You're still turning heads."

"Really, Adam?" she said shyly.

Her grandson nodded.

Delilah sighed. "I don't notice them."

"I think this is the first time you've noticed the person giving you the looks."

She walked away from Adam and went to look for her purse, as if her looking for her purse could put some distance between what had been said and her thoughts about it.

"Robert travels a lot, and so his efforts to court me may all be for nothing. I appreciate you coming out here to make sure I'm okay."

"Can we stop for a minute?"

Delilah saw concern on Adam's face. "Boy, why are you looking all pained?"

"I think Robert is different. No one is good enough for you, but he is a decent guy. I know you were happy with grandpa, and I know things weren't always perfect with mom and us, but no matter what you want, we're here for you."

Delilah stared at Adam, surprised by how moved he was. While Adam resembled his grandfather, the similarities stopped there. Her grandson wasn't afraid to put his emotions out there when it was important, and he thought her relationship with Robert was important.

Delilah went to Adam and stretched her hand out for him to take. "Right now, you are making a big deal out of it."

Her grandson smiled. "In all situations, I like to be proactive and not reactive."

Delilah blew out a breath. "If this were a business deal, I'd say you were on the right track, but it's not. The truth is, I need to come to terms with some things, and those things take time. So while I appreciate you offering help, right now, I need to swim alone."

Adam didn't seem pleased with that answer. "Until you say so, Robert's fate rests in the hands of the best grandma on the planet."

"Whatever," Delilah scoffed. "*Now* I'm the best, but I remember when you were a boy…."

Adam pulled her into his embrace. "Can't recall those times," he said, laughing. "Remember I love you."

Delilah hugged him back harder. "I love you more."

———————

"I think his work is amazing," Cassandra said at lunch. "His carvings have a life of their own. His new pieces have moving parts that give them an extra bit of depth. The one with the mother and child rocking has already sold out."

Delilah nodded and took a sip of her sweet tea. Oh, how today's youth could get stirred up when their passions were involved. They'd already gone back and forth over plans and how they would be laid out in the new woodworking house on the Cade farm. Delilah had brought up new designs and possible marketing they could use. All of it was focused around the woodworkers' representative, Evan Sparrow.

The waitress brought a plate of chicken fingers and dip. As Cassandra went on about Evan's talent, Delilah picked up a knife and cut a tender into three pieces before putting one on her plate.

"I don't think that's in the rule book."

Smiling, Cassandra nodded toward the plate. "You need to eat them with your hands."

She reached for a tender and then dunked it in the dip. "What happens if you want sauce on the whole chicken tender? You double dunk. If you had cut it up, this wouldn't be an option. I won't bother to cut this one because I can just use the dipping sauce in this container and then call for another one for you." She waved down a different waitress to get her to bring Delilah her own sauce.

"I suppose it's another way to do it."

Cassandra grinned. "Change. It sneaks up on us every time. Now, what was I saying before we discussed the proper way to eat a chicken tender?"

Delilah dipped her precut tender into her sauce. "I believe you were waxing on about the unending talent and creativity of one Evan Sparrow."

Cassandra chuckled. "I guess I was, but I'm sure you find yourself waxing these days over your new beau?"

Delilah stopped and glanced up. "My new beau?"

Cassandra's smile slipped, and she looked down at her plate. "I'm sorry. I just thought—"

Delilah closed her eyes and took a deep breath. Cassandra had only said what everyone in Sweet Blooms must be thinking. "I can't blame you for saying or thinking Robert is my new beau. In truth, I'm not sure what he is to me right now."

"Well, it sounds like, if nothing else, he's sincere. It's also good that you two can talk," she said, sounding forlorn.

Delilah clearly wasn't the only one having troubles with men. She cleared her throat. "You and Evan are…?"

Cassandra shook her head. "I can't even tell

you if he's interested in me. Some days he's complimenting me on my bone structure, and others he doesn't even notice when I walk into the room."

Delilah sympathized with the young woman and the road of indecision and insecurity she was traveling. Funny, how Delilah was almost double Cassandra's age, and here she was having the same issues and feelings. She really had to examine her situation. Robert wasn't indecisive or unclear. In fact, as soon as he said something, he made sure all parties understood. Right now, that was the problem. She completely understood what Robert wanted.

Delilah patted Cassandra's hand. "Not all guys are confident enough to be able to say what they want and how they feel. But if all of the other things you see in him show him to be a good man, wait for him."

"Maybe?" Cassandra sighed. "I'm not looking for a relationship. We're so different anyway. Besides, how odd would that be: the artist and the accountant?"

"I think you should give him a chance, if that is what you want to do."

Cassandra drew a deep breath. "Let me think about it. However, in other, more current news, are you going to give Robert a chance?" Delilah stopped and took a deep contemplative breath. What should she say?

"We're friends."

"I know a trellis that says he wants to be way more."

Delilah smiled when she thought about the trellis. "Maybe, but I need to be sure."

"I understand that one more than most, but don't wait too long," Cassandra said quietly. "Sometimes, you can lose it all if you do."

———

Whoever was at the door was going to get a piece of Delilah's mind. It was seven p.m., and she had just gotten home thirty minutes ago. After she'd walked in, she'd run out and walked Peaches. They had just gotten back, and Peaches, on the couch, was looking at the door. She raised her square head and, curious to see who was there, perked up her ears. She wasn't interested enough to get off the couch, but enough to raise her head from her relaxed pose.

The bell rang again. Delilah made sure she had a kind expression as she pulled open the door. A woman she had never seen before stood outside. She was about five foot five, with a round frame and short, straw-brown hair that lay limp around her face.

"My name is Mrs. Cordero. I'm from the shelter," she said. "I've come to assess the foster premises. Since Peaches failed her last socialization test, we wanted to make sure her environment wasn't contributing to her lack of success."

Delilah's first instinct was to slam the door in the woman's face. When Peaches had been on the side and on her way to being euthanized, no one had seemed to care, but here Mrs. Cordero was. "It's good to meet you. Please come in."

Mrs. Cordero's brow lifted, probably because she'd heard the saccharin falseness in Delilah's voice. Despite that, Delilah welcomed the woman into her home.

"She's on the couch?" Mrs. Cordero asked.

"Yes. I let her stay there because she gets lonely, and I read while she's next to me."

"You're part of the Cade family?"

"Yes."

The assessor walked into her living room and then looked around. Delilah tried to see what the assessor saw, but gave up. The woman's mouth seemed to be turning downward as she took in the room.

"You have a fireplace but no child guard? Surely, with all the money attributed to the Cades, you could have this safety feature installed for the pet you're fostering. Does Peaches ever get burned?"

Delilah was insulted. "No, she doesn't. Peaches is very smart, and we're always together in the evening. In the daytime, she's outside, where she can get fresh air, until I get home to walk her."

"The house doesn't appear to be dog-proofed. Since Peaches is a senior, she might not get into a lot, but the place should be dog-proofed."

Delilah had to pause, because she hadn't thought about dog-proofing her home. Peaches was always with her. Maybe…. No. She wasn't the one to be judged. Delilah had run into other people who had judged her based on her wealth or her name. That seemed to be the case here.

Delilah folded her arms and eyed the assessor. "Excuse me, Mrs. Cordero. Exactly why did you pay me a visit? Are you here to help Peaches socialize, or are you here to criticize me and what you perceive to be my financial status?"

Mrs. Cordero appeared shocked by the words. The woman was used to looking down her nose at others, but not anyone answering back.

"N-no, not at all. I'm here for Peaches," the assessor stammered.

Delilah went back to the couch and sat down beside Peaches. "Please take a seat in the chair. Peaches is a friendly dog, but very sensitive to my emotions, and I wouldn't want her to perceive you as anything other than someone trying to help."

Mrs. Cordero sat in the seat across the way. She pulled a small notebook from her pocketbook. "We realized when Peaches was brought in that her temperament didn't seem stable. When the tester saw her, she wasn't interactive or alert."

Delilah turned to the pit bull and simulated a kiss. Peaches raised her head and licked her cheek. Smiling, Delilah faced the assessor. "Peaches is very affectionate with me."

"I can see that she is, but that's not going to be helpful in her new-found home."

"I thought if she learned how to be affectionate with me, I could introduce her to other people, and she'd learn to trust again."

Mrs. Cordero nodded. "We must be very careful with the breed as well. Extra care has to be taken to document anything that might upset her. It's the policy that if we receive pit bulls over seven years of age, they must be put down, because the liability is too high."

"Even if the dogs haven't done anything?" Delilah asked.

Cordero shrugged. "Why wait until they misbehave? Other dogs of this same breed have turned, so Peaches is judged under the same rules as them."

Delilah held on to Peaches a little tighter. Mrs. Cordero continued to ask questions that Delilah answered as completely as she could. An hour and five treats later, the assesor left.

Delilah curled up on the sofa with Peaches. "Did you hear that lady say she thought you were just like every other pit bull? She doesn't know you. You are super cute and super smart."

The dog looked at Delilah while she spoke, and when she'd finished, Peaches gave Delilah's chin a few licks. Delilah hugged the pit bull tight. Judging Peaches by other dogs that had come before her was unfair. Fear was an issue, but if fear had been allowed to lead the way, Delilah would have missed the opportunity to be with Peaches. The dog would still be on the side, or worse, she would be gone. Again, Delilah nuzzled Peaches' head, while she thought about fair chances and pushing fear out of the equation.

Chapter Eleven

"When Mrs. Cordero first arrived, I just wanted to kick her out," Delilah said with a scowl. Robert had brought her home, and she had made them hamburgers and fries. Peaches sat waiting for the scraps that miraculously appeared under the table. "The shelter could at least have had the decency to tell me an assessor was coming."

Sitting in her kitchen, Robert saw how animated she was getting about yesterday's event. The kitchen was like her: warm and bright.

"I'm sure the shelter has a good reason for doing things that way," he said. "With all of the controversy about pit bulls, they can't be too cautious when it comes to people getting dogs."

"Then they should have done all of their checkings before they let me take Peaches home. That woman was going to pick me over like a fine tooth comb. To boot, I don't think she would have treated me the same way if my last name wasn't Cade."

"I'm sorry, Delilah. I'd like to tell you it was an anomaly, but people are people in the city and in small towns. You find good and bad everywhere."

"True." Delilah smiled. "I think you find more good if you look."

Robert smiled back. "I hope so."

Delilah passed a piece of hamburger under the table and ran into his hand. "I see I'm not the only one giving treats to Peaches. I'm sure that isn't on the recommended list of socializing her."

"Maybe not, but what can you do when you see her? It's a tough line to walk: to foster her and not spoil her as if she were your own."

Delilah nodded at the thought. He hit closer and closer to the point that had crossed her mind. What if Peaches could be hers? "After Mrs. Cordero and I got past the awkwardness, I did feel bad. I mean, she came to check on Peaches. I might not like her attitude or approach, but I do respect what she did. And yes, to answer the question, I have thought about keeping Peaches."

"Are you thinking about staying in town that long?"

"Of course!"

Robert shrugged. "You are in this rental, and…."

Delilah laughed. "Okay, smarty. I'm staying, just like you are. Is that better?"

Robert nodded. "Oh, it seems like we are going somewhere."

"Were you concerned that we weren't going anywhere?"

"Delilah, I'm human. I plan, and then I wait."

She finished eating a fry. "I look at you, and I see you being so sure. I'd never associate you with doubt. Let me help you. I'm hoping it works out and we make it back to the trellis, too."

"I'm nervous, but with that kind of encouragement, I'm also thrilled."

"Now that I've removed the doubt, what's the plan?" she joked.

Robert grinned. "Let's start with trust."

Delilah's eyes popped wide open. "Well, let's not start with anything small. Okay, trust. What about it?"

"Ask me any question you want."

Delilah paused while putting a fry in her mouth. "Any question? That's a tall order. Do I get more than one, or only one magic question?"

"I'm in a good mood. You get to ask to your heart's content."

"Okay." Delilah knew all the questions she wanted to ask. "Have you ever come close to be being married?"

"No, not really."

"Not really?"

Robert sighed. "Marriage means you are willing to compromise. I wanted a woman to fit into my life, so no, I wasn't close. I wasn't ready."

"Have you ever been tempted to be with someone outside of a committed relationship?"

He studied her for a moment. "When I look back at my life, I have been committed to my work and to the service of my country more than any woman. Have I ever cheated? No. I always felt like I was cheating on my work in previous relationships. I'm not looking for any other woman but you, Delilah."

"Last one before I let you go."

Robert smiled. "Go for it!"

"What is it about me that makes you so sure I'm the one? I know you've said some things before, but you built a trellis and basically said you wanted a long-term relationship in Sweet Blooms. In small-town language, that means marriage. Why?"

"One of the things that really attracted me to you was that you don't suffer fools. You say what you think without being mean or malicious to others."

"That's it?"

He pushed his plate away and stared into her eyes. "No. That was me stalling while I try to find a way to explain to a woman I care about why I do."

Delilah pushed her plate to the side and waited. His hands on the table were larger than hers, more rugged, and had faint scars as well as a callus or two. His nails were trimmed and clean. What would this man who had been places and experienced things see in her that would be so desirable?

"Delilah Cade, I think you are a beautiful woman inside and out. I know you've been told you're attractive. I think your characteristics are attractive. You're honest, giving, and forgiving. You bring value to everyone you meet. I've heard how you've counseled Cassandra, helped Adam in business, and even assisted Hannah. Most of all, you value family. I don't have any left, so I know how precious it is to have them and how quickly you can lose them. You were willing to move to Sweet Blooms for your family. In short, I think you are an amazing package.

Since I've been fortunate enough to find you, I'd like to keep you."

Delilah blinked away the tears that had threatened to fall. "I hope—"

Robert's phone rang. She glanced at it, and so did he. When he looked at the screen, he closed his eyes.

Delilah was more than a little curious who could call and interrupt their evening. "A problem?"

"Unfortunately. It has to be, for me to get this call."

Robert picked up his cell. "Yes, Evan, what's the issue?"

Robert's expression went from annoyed to truly concerned.

"Who said that?" After a few minutes of listening, he said: "I'll take care of it. Don't panic." Robert ended the call and then looked at her.

"I'm so sorry, Delilah. There's a problem with the guild and the guys selling their crafts. I have to go."

She wanted him to stay, but he wouldn't leave unless the matter was important. She hoped it worked out. Hearing Evan's name made her think about Cassandra. When they got to the front door, Robert gave Delilah a quick kiss on the forehead and then left.

Back in the kitchen, she looked at the two plates and then at Peaches. "Here we go."

———————

The next day, Delilah had to take the day off to care for Peaches. She rushed the dog to the vet, only to find Peaches had caught a cold. It was common and non-life-threatening, but Delilah opted to stay home with her. She took the pit bull for her walks, gave her boiled chicken, and then let her sleep on the bed. In the back of her mind, Delilah heard Mrs. Cordero saying this wasn't the way to socialize Peaches, and that she was spoiling her. Delilah ignored the criticism and went right on taking care of Peaches. When the doorbell rang, Delilah thought she had conjured up the assessor. To her relief, she opened the door to see Robert.

"Evening," he said. "How's Peaches, and is this a good time?"

Stepping back to allow him entrance, she nodded. "Peaches is asleep in my bed. When the doorbell rang, I was sure I'd be facing the shelter police or, at a minimum, Mrs. Cordero, who'd come to tell me I was spoiling Peaches."

Delilah led him to the kitchen and then made them some coffee. When she placed the cups on the table, he picked up her hand and kissed it. "Thank you."

How could a simple thing like a kiss rattle her? She sat and waited for him to start.

"Last night when I was here, Evan called me. He and all of the guys who want to be in the guild received a notice that they couldn't sell their items if they joined the guild."

"What? How can that be?"

Robert put his hands around the coffee cup and looked into it. "I went to the mayor. Sandra Waters filed a complaint with the board. She claims that when Adam's woodworking shop opens, it will take business away from her shop."

"There's got to be another way to address this issue." Delilah linked her fingers with his. This was the first time she had reached out to take his hand. Could he feel her quickened pulse at her wrist? She waited for feelings of guilt or even betrayal as she held Robert's hand, but those feelings didn't come. She might have been scared, but maybe she was ready to move on with her life and be more than Mrs. Cade.

"The mayor provided an option, but we have to see if we can make it work. Her option is for the crafters to do a certain number of classes at the center so everyone won't just go to Adam's place."

Delilah had thought she would see some relief in Robert's expression. "I'm hearing there might be a solution, but your face says nothing has changed."

Robert sighed. "A lot of the crafters don't like to be in town. They live on the outer reaches of Sweet Blooms, and some actually live in swamp areas. Getting the men to come into town and then teach classes is problematic at best. Besides, we all know that everyone can't teach."

Delilah agreed. "Have you met with the crafters?"

"I have. They made a counter offer."

She leaned forward. "I'm intrigued."

"I was too. They refused to teach in the center, but they'll send Evan to teach in town since he has the most popular items."

"Sounds like a great idea," Delilah said.

"I agree. Now, if Evan had been in the room or his colleagues had asked him before they made that offer, it would have been even better."

"Ouch!"

"I didn't use that word, but let's say it was close."

Delilah squeezed his fingers. "Should I get Cassandra to ask him?"

Robert smiled. He pulled her hand to his lips and held it there for a moment. "Remember what I said about you? About your characteristics that make you a helpful person? They come out in moments like these."

She and Robert discussed how he would approach Evan; the pros and cons of the situation. Delilah made more coffee and even gave him some fresh cream she had in the refrigerator. They spoke about Sandra Waters and the community center, and how Sandra had been in favor of Adam's shop until the crafters became involved. Delilah and Robert equally shared ideas, and he listened to her point of view and rationales.

She had always been the one to lend an ear. With Robert, she was more than just a receiver; he waited for and asked for her input as well. When it was time for him to go, she walked him to the door and he turned to face her.

"Thank you for being here and being you," he said.

"If it's in my head, you can have it."

Robert smiled. "With an invitation like that, how can a man not come back?"

Chapter Twelve

Delilah couldn't wait for lunchtime. Before the samples for the waiting rooms had come in, Robert had caught her and told her it was a picnic day for them. When she'd told Vihaan, he'd waved her out and told her to take her time with lunch.

Robert arrived wearing dark jeans and a blue chambray shirt. She saw some sweat stains on the shirt, but they just made him look rugged.

"I'm betting by how refreshed you look that your place isn't on generator three," he said with a smile. She didn't understand the comment, and her confusion must have shown on her face. "The generator went down," he explained, "and the air conditioner with it."

"Oh, no. No one told me."

"It's a good thing we are having lunch outside. Otherwise, I'd have to run to the house first."

Delilah took the bag from his hand and started to place the items on the picnic table. The bag had the name of a shop in town. "I'm no faint flower. I'm not going to die from a little sweat from an honest day's work."

He winked. "Again, her virtue shines through."

"Really? I don't know any woman who would turn you away just because of a little sweat."

He stared at her for a bit longer. "Keep that up, Delilah, and I'll think you're paying me a compliment."

"You don't need compliments. You have those aplenty. Eat up."

"I know you have a lot of great virtues, but that bossy one slipped under the radar."

One corner of her mouth turned up. "Too bad. You should have noticed it earlier, pre-trellis."

"A woman who has read the contract and the fine print. You never cease to amaze me."

"Did you get a chance to talk to Evan?"

"I did. He's willing, but he needs to know how the arrangement will work. The mayor said there are mandatory times for classes. So we're all still working things out."

"Just when you think the issue's resolved. I know it's going to be fine. Anything we can do?"

Robert just nodded. "This needs to be addressed by me. If either you or Adam steps in, Sandra Waters will cry foul play, and in a town this small, that will divide folks on who to support if the board calls a meeting."

Delilah nodded. "It's been a while since I've dealt with small-town politics."

"Hello, Mrs. Cade."

Mrs. Cordero?

Delilah looked straight ahead at Robert. He appeared to be trying not to smile. She closed her eyes and wished the assessor away three times. Delilah had seen a movie where if you said someone's name three times, they appeared. She wondered if it worked in reverse.

"Mrs. Cade?" Delilah could now officially say that it did not work at all in reverse. Glancing over her shoulder, she saw the rotund figure of Mrs. Cordero coming toward her. Delilah and Robert were on one side of the picnic table, so the assessor went to stand on the other.

"Hello, Mrs. Cordero," Delilah said.

Robert stood up and offered his hand. "Mrs. Cordero."

The assessor looked at him and gave him a

curt nod before turning her attention back to Delilah. "I would like to speak with you regarding Peaches. Can we have a moment alone?"

Before Delilah could speak, Robert answered: "I'm well aware of Peaches' situation."

Mrs. Cordero focused on him again. "Exactly who are you?"

"Robert Parker."

"I've heard about you in town." The assessor shook his hand and then took a seat at the picnic table. "I'm concerned for Peaches."

Delilah had to hold her tongue. "I'm not sure what the problem is."

"Well, after I reported the conditions in which Peaches is living, we all thought there were some concerns." Mrs. Cordero looked at Robert. "Mrs. Cade doesn't seem to understand the delicacy and importance of socialization when it comes to this breed."

"Is the breed the issue?" he asked. "We should look at the dog as its own individual personality."

The assessor nodded. "Of course, we take the personality into consideration. However, we also have to look at the traits of the pit bull breed."

"I agree," Robert said. "While we keep in mind the breed's possible actions, let's also make sure we are looking out for what's best for Peaches."

"Of course."

Listening to them talk reminded Delilah of a game of tennis. As soon as Mrs. Cordero said one thing, Robert countered with another. It got into a steady rhythm, and then Robert stopped the game.

"What are you trying to say to Delilah today?"

Mrs. Cordero sat up straighter. "What is your role?"

"I'm her fiancé."

The assessor nodded. Mrs. Cordero faced Delilah. "Is Robert helping you socialize Peaches?"

Delilah couldn't seem to find the words to answer; she was still in shock from hearing him say he was her fiancé. She didn't want to correct him in front of the woman, either. Delilah turned to Robert.

Smiling, he looked back at her. "Yes, I'm helping Delilah with Peaches."

Mrs. Cordero looked between the both of them. "I didn't know you had any other type of stimulation or socialization for Peaches."

Robert's smile grew as Delilah remained silent. "I have two dogs, and we're waiting for Peaches to get over her cold. I've also had extensive experience with large breed dogs."

Delilah had told him she would give him a chance, but she hadn't accepted his proposal and become his fiancée. Robert had said what he had, though, because he knew how important Peaches was to her.

"Have you seen Peaches? She's a senior dog. Her quality of life will be costly to maintain," Mrs. Cordero said.

Robert eyed the assessor. "I have seen Peaches, and I think she's a wonderful dog. We are well aware of what it means to be a senior. I assure you, between myself and Delilah, we might even be able to scrounge up a couple of pennies to take care of Peaches."

Delilah covered a laugh by discreetly coughing. She could see now what everyone was talking about when they called Robert a master planner—and why Adam had reached out to him.

Robert didn't give Mrs. Cordero a chance to answer. "You don't understand Delilah's commitment to Peaches." He pulled Delilah's hand onto the table and intertwined their fingers for the assessor to see. "Delilah saw Peaches and decided to give the dog a better life than she's had in the first half of her life. Delilah has a job, but she can work from home. She's not afraid of the breed, which you think is a big thing. Delilah is one of the most giving and loving people you could find. It's a golden opportunity for Peaches to have someone committed to her. The shelter should consider it a gift to find someone who obviously cares enough to want to help an animal for whom you had such low hopes. I'm not sure what you came to say or what you've been looking at, but Delilah and I are both committed to giving the best life possible to Peaches. We will be putting in an application to adopt her."

Delilah knew this was all for her, but she still blinked back a few tears. Of course, she had heard him talk about her attributes and goodness.

To hear him speak of her in such glowing terms to someone else was humbling in a way she hadn't known she needed.

Mrs. Cordero looked between Robert and Delilah. She sighed and stood up. "I'm sorry I wasn't aware of all of the facts before I came out here. I initially came to say that the shelter had reviewed the situation and thought it might be better for Peaches to come back and be around a more experienced handler." She smoothed nonexistent wrinkles from her pants. "However, I can see you have addressed the issue. You, Robert, have prior experience with dogs, and you are correct; I can see from the effort Mrs. Cade has put in that she is dedicated and truly cares for Peaches. I'll also make a note that you wish to permanently home Peaches. If you two will excuse me, I'll leave you to your lunch."

Mrs. Cordero walked away and left a silence Delilah had no idea how to address. Delilah needed to thank him for all he'd said, but where did she start?

"You didn't have to go out on a limb like that," she said once she'd finally gathered her thoughts.

"There was no limb to go out on." He released her hand and went back to eating. "Peaches is a lot like family to you."

Delilah smiled and nodded as she returned to her food. "She is. I hadn't realized it, but it's true. I'm getting used to hearing the patter of her feet on the floor. The feel of her wet nose, too, when she's waking me up to take her out."

"Mrs. Cordero is trying to do what is right, or at least, I'm hoping she's trying to do the right thing by the dogs. Seems like she doesn't have any experience with someone like you."

"Like me?"

"Yes. Someone willing to fight for family and make lifestyle adjustments for them. Peaches isn't an inconvenience for you. Peaches is just Peaches."

Delilah swallowed and had to keep herself from tearing up. He understood exactly how she felt about Peaches. As if he could read her mind, he faced her, and then he set his hand beneath her chin.

"Look at me, Delilah," he whispered.

She did, and they stared into one another's eyes.

"I told you all the reasons I want to be with you," he said. "Those were just the biggest attributes, not the only ones. You are a rare jewel, and I'm grateful for every day that I'm with you. No matter what happens, even though I'm planning for the best outcome, if it doesn't work out the way that

I want, you've still made a change in my life."

Delilah gave a short nod. Robert traced her jawline and caressed her cheek before his hand fell away.

"Know that I not only care about you, but I also respect who you are and value your opinions." With that, he turned back to his food and started talking about the finer parts of the project that still had to be addressed.

She nodded and even answered some questions, but she did so half-heartedly. It came to her clear as a sunny day and hit her like a ton of bricks: She was truly and deeply in love with this man.

———

Robert hated that all of the work he had put into the guild was being laid on Evan's shoulders. Robert had a meeting scheduled with the mayor. Even though Evan had said yes to teaching after receiving and reading the terms from the mayor, Robert wanted to make sure the craftsman understood exactly what was being asked of him.

Evan hadn't wanted to meet on the Cade site, so they were meeting at Robert's place. When Robert heard the dogs bark and then go silent, he knew Evan had arrived. The man had a way about him when it came to animals and children. Evan brought calm to situations and to the people around him. Robert opened the door and invited the craftsman in.

"Hello, Evan."

"Parker."

Robert had black coffee waiting and some biscuits from Geeta. When he'd told Delilah about meeting with Evan, she had smiled and given him the biscuits. "I thought you might need these. A little birdie told me he likes them." Robert had thanked her for being there for him again. She was always proving herself to be more giving than the last time.

Evan walked in and went straight to the kitchen. He had on his typical wear: a T-shirt and blue jeans that still had wood dust on them. Evan helped himself to some coffee. He took a seat at the table. He nodded toward the basket on the table, and Robert nodded back.

They both sat in silence for a minute, just drinking coffee and eating biscuits. Robert cleared his throat, and Evan looked up as if he had just remembered Robert was there.

"Thank you for calling me before," Robert said. "I know it was a big shock to everyone, and we all want to thank you for what you've done so far."

"No need. We're all the same, doing the same work," replied Evan.

"You know that your work sells the best?" Robert asked.

"People are weird. My work is good, but we've got better craftsmen in the group. I think the reason folks think mine is better is because I can spend all day on it. The other guys have families and small farms."

Robert agreed. "I'm not saying your thinking is wrong. I'm saying because of what the town thinks, you teaching in the community center is a big deal."

Evan grunted in agreement.

"I spoke with the mayor, and I told you about the teaching."

"Yup."

"They have a teaching schedule they want you to follow, and they need you to be available after the classes."

Evan stopped midway to putting a biscuit in his mouth. He gave Robert a confused look.

"What does that mean, to be available after classes? They want longer classes?"

Robert sat up straighter. "Evan, to be able to accommodate them, you are going to have to move to town. The owner of the community center made the case that emergencies could happen, and to ensure you can do the classes and possibly even extra classes that might come up, you need to be living in town. What are your thoughts?"

Evan sat back and tapped the handle of his cup. "I don't have a lot at my place. Where would I stay in Sweet Blooms?"

Robert let out a breath he didn't realize he'd been holding. He'd prepared to convince Evan that he had to relocate, but the craftsman hadn't even protested the move.

"I thought for sure you would object to the move, but you just asked where you would be staying."

Evan shrugged. "I'm looking at town life differently."

Robert nodded knowingly. "You're looking at town life differently or looking at someone in town differently?"

Evan shrugged. Just when Robert thought the craftsman would let the question go, he said: "I saw what you did with the trellis. More importantly, I saw the woman painting the trellis."

Robert gave Evan a surprised look. "What?"

"You didn't know? Cassandra asked me to drop off some paint before coming here. It seems your lady has decided to say yes to you in public."

Robert smiled. All day Delilah had avoided him; now he knew why.

"So you're good to move to town, Evan?"

The craftsman held up his hand. "Hold up. I need to finalize some things first. If I'm going to move to Sweet Blooms, I'll need to sell my old place so I can buy a new one in town."

"Okay. Anything else?"

"What is the pay for teaching the classes? If I have to do my own work and teach, I won't be able to make as many products. I'll need a salary from the center if they want me to teach."

"Done."

Evan nodded. He reached for a biscuit and continued to eat. When he was done with the second biscuit, he thanked Robert and left.

Robert cleared up the kitchen. He couldn't wait to tell the mayor about Evan's terms, and he couldn't wait to see the trellis in the morning. By all accounts, tomorrow was going to be a banner day.

Chapter Thirteen

Today would be the turning point in Delilah's life. When Robert saw the trellis, he'd know she was ready to commit to him, and then a new chapter in her life would begin.

When she walked into the building, she found a guest waiting for her: Clarissa Long, the town beauty queen and a member of the board. Delilah had heard about her from Hannah. Clarissa had thought her blond hair and curvaceous body would be enough to get Adam to the altar. Unease settled over Delilah, and she didn't like it one bit.

"Hello, Ms. Long," she said, placing her bag on the counter.

"Mrs. Cade." Clarissa smiled.

The beauty queen, in a high-waisted skirt with sandals and peasant shirt that flowed over her ample bosom, had dressed to impress. Her dark eyes were like an eagle's: looking for an angle. Even her mouth had a quirk; it made her look like she was always smirking.

"What can I do for you?" Delilah asked.

"Actually, I came to speak to Robert, but he's not here. I thought I could ask you about the progress in getting one of the craftsmen to live in town."

There was no rhyme or reason as to why Clarissa using Robert's first name just irked Delilah.

"I don't have an update for you."

"That's a shame." Instead of leaving like any

other normal person would, Clarissa walked around and then came back to the counter. "I'll have to try to see him later. If the trellis is any indication, you'll be staying here in Sweet Blooms?"

"Yes. I want to be here when Adam and Hannah get married."

Clarissa's smile tightened for a second, and then the beauty queen's expression brightened.

"That's such good news. I know how open-hearted Adam is, and I'm sure they'll do well together. In that vein, I guess I should be saying happy nuptials to you as well."

"Thank you."

"I hope all works out well for you. I recall a woman named Loretta, she tried to find love in her later years. She fell for a military man who traveled and saw the world. If I remember the story right, he lived in Sweet Blooms for six years, and everyone thought they were an item.

On the day they were getting engaged, he backed out.

He joined the Red Cross and asked Loretta to go. Of course, she couldn't, because her whole life was in Sweet Blooms. It was just tragic to see her after their split. She didn't go out in public for a while. Poor woman. You just never really know. When people have that travel bug, they just gotta go.

I'm just totally jealous of the vacations Robert takes. When he's not working, he's traveling and holidaying. Anyway, I'm sure you'll enjoy it. The sacrifices we make for new relationships."

Delilah gripped the counter so tightly, her hands must have imprinted on it.

"I appreciate your concern, Clarissa. Robert and I are perfectly comfortable with his traveling."

"Oh, I didn't mean to imply you might not

be his type, or that he'd leave you eventually because of the travel bug. You two seem way more in tune with one another, and it's an inspiration to see couples like you, especially mature couples, giving it a second go."

"I'm sure we'll muddle along."

"Of course, I'm only making conversation. Anyway, I'll be going now. Oh, and please let Robert know the trip to Bali he was planning is available."

Delilah fought not to do something unladylike. "You know about Robert's travel?"

Clarissa beamed; her smile almost wouldn't fit onto her face.

"I'm sorry. I thought you knew. I'm the local travel agent. I know all of his traveling spots for this year and the next three."

"The next three?"

"Yes. It's like I told you: He gets that traveling bug a lot. It's enough to make me jealous."

Clarissa left, and Delilah was determined not to get upset. While Delilah couldn't prove it, she sensed mean, vindictive, and petty Clarissa had come in just to torment her.

Had the beauty queen spoken the truth? Surely, after all the time Delilah and Robert had been together, he would have told her about his yearly traveling and upcoming plans. Had it been an oversight? Leaving her bag in the building, Delilah went outside to look at the trellis. Previously it had been only a wooden frame, but she and Cassandra had painted it white last night. Delilah had even draped some lace around it.

Now when she saw it, she wasn't so sure about Robert anymore. She wouldn't fall into a depression. She'd confront him and hear him deny what the beauty queen had said, and then it would be better.

Just when she tried to figure out how to bring up the issue, and when, Robert came toward her with a large smile on his face. She wouldn't have to wait after all.

———

Robert had seen the trellis earlier. His patience had won out. When he'd dropped some supplies outside of the house and seen Delilah gazing at the trellis, he'd figured it would be the perfect time for them to plan when they'd both be under the trellis.

As he got closer, he noticed she wasn't smiling. Had something happened with Hannah and Adam? It was still early in their engagement; too early for any major problems to have come up.

Delilah turned to him, and instead of her dazzling smile, she gave him a thoughtful look.

When he stood in front of her, her countenance didn't change.

"Delilah? Are you okay?"

"I am."

"I saw the trellis this morning. Does all the decorating mean what I think it means?"

She cocked her head to the side and held up one finger. "I've got one question for you." Robert was a little disconcerted by her tone and the way she just avoided answering the question. He had imagined this happening a lot of different ways but so far none of those scenarios were coming to pass.

Robert was getting concerned. Delilah not showing emotion signaled something was very wrong. She wouldn't meet his gaze, and she seemed tense. Something was definitely wrong. He waited; she'd tell him.

"Were you really planning on going to Bali?"

Bali. He had totally forgotten about the trip.

He had neglected to cancel. Did she want to go? "I had made some plans, but I don't think I'll be going."

"Because?"

Smiling, Robert pointed at the trellis. Delilah nodded and drew in a breath. "I thought so."

"Hey, what's going on?"

"Nothing. Nothing is going on. I was caught up in the illusion when I painted the trellis."

"Excuse me?"

"The trellis was such a grand gesture. I'd never had a man approach me in such a way. I was taken up in the moment. I don't think a relationship will work between us."

Robert felt as though he had just been punched in the kidney. The wind had been knocked out of him and he felt the signs of dizziness make him wobble. "What brought this on?"

"It's about making sure you can be you, and

you're not with a woman who hampers your nature."

"Shouldn't I be the one to say if my nature is being hampered?"

Frustration, like he had never known, built within him. Delilah was the one. He respected her, trusted her, and now, while she was trying to leave him, he could say it: He loved her. He would listen to what she said and then listen for the things she didn't say. Delilah was worth the fight.

"One day, you will say your nature was hampered. The thing is, by then, it'll be too late for me. Yes, the more I think about it, the more it makes sense for us to go separate ways. I'd love to be your friend, but I just don't think anything more would be good for either one of us."

"Things don't change like this overnight. What happened?" he asked. "Give me the chance to defend myself against it."

She blinked and looked past him. "I've told you everything already. If there's nothing for you to see, then there's nothing for you to fix."

"We are not children."

"Are you calling me a child?"

Robert took a deep breath. "Delilah—"

"No, Robert. This is best. The question you need to answer is whether we can still be friends."

"You going from the woman I want to spend the rest of my life with to just being a friend? You're right. I'll need to think about that."

Robert had no more words to give her; nothing to say that would be constructive. Instead, he did the last thing he thought he would be doing when he'd woken up this morning.

Robert Parker walked away from the woman of his dreams.

———————

Delilah sat on her couch with Peaches in her arms. She felt hollow. No other word for it: just hollow. She hadn't felt this empty when she'd become a widow. She just wanted to lie with Peaches and let the world pass her by.

She hadn't gone onsite for three days and had done all of her work through Vihaan. She had given Robert the ultimatum of being friends or nothing at all, but the way it was looking, she should have really asked herself that question. It was odd; even though she was hurt, she still didn't regret the experience. Robert had helped her to realize she was more than her past.

Now she knew she was more, and she could be having more, but she was alone. Peaches provided only temporary relief. When Delilah walked the pit bull or groomed her, then her mind became otherwise occupied, but beyond that, her thoughts went right back to Robert.

Over the last couple of days, she would go sit in the kitchen and remember the conversations they'd had. She'd remember him touching her hand. Hannah and Cassandra had asked her if she wanted to go out, but she had declined. No one wanted to be around a person who was moping. In the evening, she wondered if Robert thought about her as much as she did him.

She missed him. She didn't just miss the man trying to woo her, although she definitely missed that. She missed the friend she could bounce ideas off of. She missed her partner. Why did he need to travel?

The real problem, though, wasn't the traveling. She feared he would leave her; that something—or someone—would pull him away from her. If he had been any other person from Sweet Blooms, this issue would never have come up, but he was Robert Parker. World traveler.

Her doorbell was ringing.

She made it to the door. Cassandra stood on the other side.

"Cassandra, I'm sorry. I really—"

The woman walked in and looked at Delilah. "I'm here as a form of Red Cross."

"Excuse me?"

"Well, you haven't made it to the site, and the trellis is painted. Hannah couldn't come see you because she's holding Adam back from killing Robert."

"Oh, for goodness sake."

"I volunteered to come because I figured we could commiserate on the hardheadedness of men."

Delilah nodded.

"I take it your problem is Evan?"

Cassandra reached behind her and tied her long black hair into a top knot.

"Problem doesn't even begin to describe what is wrong with Evan. We would need a whole new session to go over his faults."

"That bad?"

Cassandra sighed. "Let's just say that at least you and Robert can talk to one another. Some days I feel like I don't know enough English to speak to Evan."

The woman walked over to the couch.

"Don't give me too much credit," Delilah said. "I thought Robert and I were both saying the same thing, but then our relationship went south."

"How? I painted the trellis with you. Everything was fine then."

Delilah let out a breath and sat down next to Peaches. She rubbed the dog's head as she snuggled up next to her. At that moment, Delilah realized how much she needed to talk to someone.

"I was okay, and then Clarissa came by—"

"Oh, no! As soon as you mentioned her name, I knew she was guilty."

Delilah smiled. "I may not have appreciated her delivery, but she still gave facts."

"We'll see. Let me hear the rest of it."

Cassandra sat with her arms over her chest. "I take it Clarissa is not your favorite person?"

The woman laughed. "Does it show?"

Delilah laughed with her. "It's been days since I've done anything but stare into space. If for nothing else, thank you."

"Come, tell me what the evil Clarissa did."

Delilah's mouth tilted upwards. "She wasn't evil. She told me about the Bali trip Robert had booked."

"Yeah," Cassandra said, "I heard he was trying to go."

"Did everyone know he had the travel bug?"

"Travel bug?"

"It doesn't matter now, so I can tell you. A deal-breaker for me in a relationship is a person who needs to travel and leave me behind. I thought I had talked about it with Robert, but when Clarissa told me about the trip, and I asked him, he didn't think it was a big deal."

Cassandra held up her hands. "Let me see if I have this straight. You were upset because you believed Robert needed to travel alone. When he didn't tell you about the trip, you saw it as a sign he would always travel and leave you behind?"

Delilah nodded. "See? You understand!"

Cassandra's expression didn't show agreement or understanding. Instead, she looked a little sad.

"You're the one who doesn't understand, Delilah. He told you the truth. The Bali trip is with the community center. His traveling friends wanted to go, and picked a bunch of exotic places, but Clarissa wanted Robert to go for free, to be a guide, because he had been to the place already. He wasn't going because of the desire to travel. He'd be helping out the community center."

Delilah covered her face with her hands. Now she felt like crying.

"Was I really that foolish and scared?"

Cassandra rubbed her back, and Peaches rubbed her head against her. After another hour had passed, during which the Cassandra explained the details, Cassandra left. Delilah stood with her back against the door. Peaches ran to the door with her leash.

She took the leash from the dog's mouth.

"First we take you for your walk. Then I must go and find a way to grovel to your new master."

Chapter Fourteen

Robert had to face the truth. Delilah didn't want him or what he had to offer.

After setting down his toolkit, he touched the trellis and smiled at the white paint. He'd thought his wooing of Delilah had been going well, and then it hadn't been. Sleep hadn't come easy to him last night and the thought of eating wasn't something he looked forward to but he did because he knew his body needed feul but what his heart needed wasn't available to him.

He wasn't one to wallow in regret. He'd had his share of disappointments. His relationship with Delilah was bigger than the rest, but he'd live, just not happily. He had survived the war, the death of his family, and the deaths of most of his friends. Truth was, he would survive this too.

The woodworkers' hall would soon be complete. The crew were putting in the cosmetic parts. All of them had Delilah's touch. The final straw would be when the building was ready this week. No sense in carrying on what couldn't be.

"Did you come out here to build a bigger one? I mean, if you did, that would really hurt the rest of the men in Sweet Blooms."

Robert turned to see Adam. Delilah's grandson was the last person he wanted to talk to right now, but Adam was still the boss, and this was still Adam's land.

"A man's got to know when to cut his losses."

"He's also got to hold fast when dealing with female interference."

Robert turned around, confused. Adam smiled.

"You have no idea what that means. Neither do I, but Hannah sent me out here with that phrase, and I wanted to make sure it wasn't just me having a problem with it."

"Adam, I'm not sure why you're here."

"Well, officially, I'm not. Unofficially, my wife told me to fix this."

Robert was still confused.

"Let me start again. I heard you and Delilah were on the outs due to no fault of either one of you. Then I come out here, and you've got a toolbox. I can only assume you plan on taking down the trellis. Are you thinking of leaving town?"

"Delilah is a very special woman. I don't want anything around that might cause her discomfort. The trellis was my pitch, and it failed. I know when to take my ball and go home, so to speak, and I'm doing that with as little fanfare as I can possibly manage."

"That brings us to why we're talking now. You need to speak to Delilah."

Robert blinked. "I don't know how up to date your information is, but she asked if we could be friends. I'm not looking for that."

Adam cringed. "Not the friends conversation."

When Robert remembered her trying to explain how the decision to be made was about friendship, he tensed up. "Yes, she gave me the friends talk. She and I are done."

"What if I told you the reason you grew horns in a day is because of Clarissa?"

Robert stopped and looked at the younger man. When he heard the name he had a flare up of anger but he put it to the side. It was more important to get the facts here. "I'm listening."

Adam told him about the exchange in the

building, and then he stopped, sighed and shook his head. "It's my understanding Delilah's been looking for you to tell you she was wrong and she's sorry. She wants to be more than friends." Adam shook his head. "This conversation is just so wrong on so many levels for me."

Robert laughed. "I'm glad you came by. You've made everything clear." He turned back to the trellis and took out his tools.

"Hey, are you still leaving?"

"Nope."

"Then what are you doing?"

"If what you said earlier was true, I'm about to up the bar for the rest of the men in Sweet Blooms."

————————

In the room with the mayor, Sandra Waters was a different woman. The welcoming, nice demeanor she had at the community center was tucked away to let out the shrewd businesswoman.

"Hello, Mr. Parker. I wanted to personally facilitate this meeting between you and Ms. Waters," Mayor Mason said, sitting at the round table. Robert suspected she'd chosen the round table on purpose: It had no head and was a perfect sphere.

"We're in Sweet Blooms. You can call me Robert."

Sandra nodded at him and then the mayor.

The mayor sighed. "Okay, let's address the business at hand." She then held out her hand for Sandra's handout. "Let's keep this civil and about business."

Sandra held up her hands. "Of course."

Robert sensed tension between the two women, but he obviously wasn't going to be made privy to those details.

The mayor cleared her throat. "Sandra gave us projections about how the woodhouse would affect her business. The numbers seemed correct, and we brought the problem to you. It appears we have a solution. Is that correct, Robert?"

"Yes, it is, but can I see the projections again?"

"Of course."

Robert looked them over and then gave them back to the mayor. "We can accommodate the potential loss. We've asked Evan Sparrow if he will teach. We've also gotten him to move into town as long as suitable arrangements can be found."

Sandra narrowed her eyes. "Suitable arrangements?"

Robert nodded. "He's selling his place to live here. The board will need to buy his property so he can get another one."

"That's outrageous!" Sandra countered.

Robert smiled. "It's part of the bargain. It shouldn't be an issue if you are really going to suffer the loss outlined in that report."

Sandra's lips tightened, and the mayor glanced to the side and discreetly coughed.

"Sandra, Robert is correct; we should have no problem absorbing the expense if the future gains are as you say."

"Of course. I just didn't want to be presumptuous about what the board could absorb," she said shrewdly.

The mayor nodded. "Good. Now that that's taken care of, please extend our thanks to Evan Sparrow for taking on the position."

Sandra cleared her throat. "From now on,

it would be best if Mr. Sparrow came to the table to negotiate on his own."

"Ah," Robert said. "Do you think I suggested the buying of the house?"

Sandra raised her eyebrow. "Mr. Sparrow is not as familiar with our rules as you might be. I'm just suggesting he should represent himself to make sure his concerns are met. I'd also like to suggest another crafter be allowed to teach. His name is Barrick."

"Barrick isn't someone I'd choose to teach," Robert said.

"Why not? I know you haven't spent time with him, because he approached me separately. He indicated he hadn't been given a fair chance, and that only Evan was asked."

The mayor cleared her throat and looked at Robert. "Is that true?"

He stared at the smug Sandra Waters and fought indecision. Instead of falling into the quagmire of doubt he pushed aside his feelings and then began to dissect the situation and itemize what he knew to be true. Barrick didn't have the right temperament to be around too many people. Teaching was hard work, and Barrick was a little rougher around the edges than even Robert preferred. The problem was, he needed to make a decision that would ease the rest of the negotiations.

"Fine. We can try Barrick, if that's what you'd prefer to do. We should go slowly, though, because we haven't talked to Barrick about what would be best for the guild.

Sandra sniffed. "That's just another way of saying you haven't had in-depth talks with him, as you have with Evan."

Robert smiled. "I am not opposed to Evan coming in to negotiate, but you might find he doesn't negotiate the same way you do. It was Evan's idea, not mine, to sell his house in the swamp and get a new one in town. When he mentioned the idea to me, he didn't pose it as a question." Robert stood and nodded to the mayor. "Be careful of the prejudices you apply to people before you know them. Good day, ladies."

———————

At the shelter, Delilah sat in Mrs. Cordero's office. The assessor had called her and left several messages saying she needed to come to the shelter about Peaches. If Mrs. Cordero's desk was any indication of the person then Delilah was surprised anything got done. The desk was a mess with cluttered paperwork everywhere.

In the background she could hear the faint barking of dogs and she was sad when Delilah thought about it could be Peaches. As she waited for Mrs. Cordero to arrive her palms were sweaty and she began randomly tapping her feet to some unknown beat.

The last two days had been one disappointment after another. On Monday, when she'd gone to find Robert, he hadn't been on site. When she'd gone in the next day, the office was solemn, and even Vihaan seemed down. When she'd asked why, he hadn't answered. That afternoon, she'd gone out for some air and then she'd known: The trellis was gone.

She had waited too long. Pride had kept her from leaving tons of messages on his cellphone and at his job site. She hadn't bothered to hamper the tears that had fallen down her face. For a long while, she'd stayed looking at the spot where the trellis had once been. That night, she'd gone home and cried with Peaches in her arms. Her grief had been so intense, she'd been sick that night and hadn't been able to eat.

In the morning, she'd resolved to find a way to make it to the end of the week. All of her work was done, and there'd be a party in the main building to celebrate the end of the project, but she wasn't sure she'd even attend. A small part of her said she had to go. It might be the last time she saw Robert. Then Mrs. Cordero had called. Delilah had avoided answering her back, because it would be too much for her to have to give up Peaches too.

In the office at the shelter, Delilah was on pins and needles waiting to find out what Mrs. Cordero wanted. Finally, the assessor came in and took a seat.

"I want to apologize for our last meeting," she began.

Shocked, Delilah nodded in acknowledgment, and Mrs. Cordero shuffled through some papers on her desk. While Delilah didn't know exactly what the woman was sorry about, this wasn't the time for Delilah to push her luck.

As if she knew Delilah wouldn't reply, Mrs. Cordero continued: "I was overzealous in my concern for Peaches when I first came to your house. I visited to check on socialization, which you were addressing in a measured way suitable for a dog her age. I was wrong," she finished quietly.

Delilah's confusion deepened. "Thank you for telling me."

"I also wanted you to know that I reviewed my actions and the evaluation of Peaches and determined yours would be a suitable home for Peaches."

Both joy and abysmal grief ran though Delilah. Her home would have been a great place for Peaches if Delilah were still with Robert.

"Do you know the current status of my relationship with Mr. Parker? Was us being a couple a factor in the adoption approval?" Delilah waited with bated breath.

Mrs. Cordero waved away her concerns. "Mr. Parker already came in and brought his dogs as well, so yes, they've all been cleared by the shelter to be with one another. If you will just sign some paperwork, you will be the new owner of Peaches."

Robert had already been here? With his dogs? He had updated the assessor on their situation. Delilah wanted to ask Mrs. Cordero some questions, because it seemed like she knew more than Delilah right now, but the woman had left the room. When she returned, she had a handful of paperwork.

"If you will sign on the lines marked with the red x, we will be all done, and Peaches will be yours."

Delilah nodded and took the pile of papers. On the first page, she found the **x**. Robert's signature was already there as co-owner. As she flipped through the papers to find the signature lines, she continually found Robert's already there. He had made it possible for her to adopt Peaches.

Another thing he had done that put him a cut above the rest. She blinked back tears. After signing the last paper, Delilah passed the pile back to Mrs. Cordero.

The assessor looked the documents over and then held out her hand. Delilah took it in a firm grasp.

"Congratulations, Mrs. Cade. You are now the proud owner of Peaches."

Delilah smiled and thanked Mrs. Cordero, but when she got into her car, she laid her head on the steering wheel. She had Peaches, but no Robert. If only she could have them both.

Chapter Fifteen

Delilah went to the Cade ranch. It was the final day to finish up last-minute paperwork; a great time to go in and avoid the pitying stares. Delilah didn't know if the crew really looked at her with those stares, but she'd been feeling sorry for herself lately. It would pass, but for now, she was not at her best. When she got to her building, she opened the door and saw a man with a bag standing there; he appeared to be scavenging her supplies.

"Hello?"

The man stopped and looked at her.

He waved her off. "I don't need help.

I'm supposed to be here," he said defensively.

"My name is Mrs. Cade. Are you a crafter? If you are looking for Robert, you're in the wrong building."

"I don't want him! He doesn't want me to get the same things he's giving Evan."

The man wasn't taller than Delilah, but he had more muscle than she did. Besides that, the fidgety way he moved made her nervous.

"Are you here with Evan?"

"No! Evan is getting more than the rest of us. I spoke to the lady, Sandra. She told me they would give him somewhere to live and food. All he had to do was make the same things we're making. I can do the same thing."

Delilah reached into her pocketbook and palmed her phone. She looked down for a moment to put in her code and then hit redial. The last person she had tried to reach was Robert in a moment of weakness. She had let the phone ring once, and no one had answered. When she glanced down now, she saw he had picked up. She shook her head; that was just her luck.

"Look, mister. I don't even know your name, but I think you are in the wrong building."

The guy shook his head. "The Waters woman told me I could get supplies."

After what seemed like forever, the door opened.

"Barrick, is that you?" *Robert.*

It was surreal to hear his voice. She had been trying to talk to him to make things better, and she had been thwarted at every attempt. Disappointment and anger seeped in. If he picked up the phone and came when she was in trouble, then he had been around the whole time. He had been purposely avoiding her! Better to stew in the anger than to wallow in the pain of how far he had gone to avoid her.

"That you, Parker?"

"Yes, it is." Robert steadily walked toward the man named Barrick. As Robert came towards them she felt thrilled to see him again, grateful that he had showed up and overall awed by his handsomeness. If ever there was a time, he had picked the right one to be the knight in shining armor.

"I-it's not what it looks like." Barrick glanced from side to side. "The Waters woman said you were okay with me coming here. She said I could get supplies, and you'd give me things just like Evan."

"I don't give Evan things. He earns them from the crafts he makes," Robert said.

Barrick seemed to be getting desperate. She looked at the size difference between the men. They were roughly the same height, but Barrick appeared wider and bigger. She wanted to cry out and tell Robert to stop moving toward him, but she didn't want to distract him.

Barrick shuffled to and fro. "I'm here because Waters said it was okay."

Robert moved close enough to touch Barrick, and the next thing Delilah knew, Barrick was on the floor.

"I didn't do anything!"

"You shouldn't have been here. I spoke with Waters. You don't have anything to pick up."

"Evan gets things. It's not fair! Evan gets things!"

Robert looked over his shoulder. "Delilah, call Adam. Tell him to call the sheriff."

She ran to the house and called Adam. She tried to wait around to make sure Robert was okay, but Adam told her it would be a long night. There'd be questions for Sandra Waters; they must find out exactly what she had promised Barrick.

When Delilah managed to catch Robert's eye,

he told her he'd see her in the morning. The words were like a salve to a bleeding wound. The how didn't matter. What mattered: She would see Robert in the morning, and one way or another, she would be able to find some closure.

———

When she heard the bell, she was up and dressed in her best sunflower dress. Delilah didn't know what was about to happen, but she'd look good when it did. The doorbell rang again, and she measured her steps to get to the door. She didn't want to appear desperate.

"Delilah, it's me, Robert."

She had her hand on the door. These were the final moments. Once she pulled the door open, the wait would be over.

Her hand shook. Maybe she should tell him she was ill and to come back tomorrow, when she had a plan to deal with all the possibilities? No. Fear had cost her enough and caused her enough pain. She'd gather all of her courage and hope for the best.

She yanked open the door. The first thing that came to mind was that the man looked good in the morning, and he looked good in the evening. Oh, yes. She was very happy with her choice of sundress and matching sandals.

He took her in from head to toe, and a smile broke out across his face, transforming him from good-looking to looking amazing. "Is there a woman in his house who would entertain being a bit more than friends?" he asked as he stepped across the threshold.

"You're in luck. It just so happens that the friend window has closed, but the fiancée window has opened for a limited time only."

She closed the door and turned to find his arms wide open.

"Is it that easy?" she asked.

Robert laughed. "I'm too old to be holding anything that doesn't make me feel good. If you're willing, then I'm still here."

She went into his arms and sank in his embrace. He kissed the top of her head. "I'm sorry," she mumbled against his chest.

"You let Clarissa muddy the waters. We have to be able to go to each other, Delilah. I'm not here with you because I'm on furlough. I'm also not in my twenties and thirties anymore, where stopping by a gal in port is good for a break, and then I need to hit the road again."

She eyed him with suspicion. "You knew it was Clarissa because…?"

"Because you are surrounded by at least a dozen people whose only concern is to make sure you are happy. I've heard a lot about Clarissa, but nothing good. It seems she is always wreaking havoc."

Delilah laughed. "I'd have to agree. I want to say it's because Adam chose Hannah instead of her, but she has the kind of meanness that has to fester for a long time."

Robert leaned back and caressed her cheek. "We have to agree to never let anyone come between us. We should give each other the benefit of the doubt; at least present the problem to the other party to dispute."

"Agreed," Delilah said. "Well, since we are still an item, I made biscuits and coffee."

The corners of Robert's mouth went up. "If we hadn't worked things out?"

"Then I would have taken my biscuits to Adam, and they would have eaten them. However, since you've shown such good sense, I can feed you."

Both of them laughed as they went into the kitchen.

Delilah served coffee, and after a biscuit or

two, she saw something was weighing on Robert.

"We just got back together, but you look weighed down."

Robert sighed. "I'm glad this part of my life is going well. I'm just thinking of Barrick."

Delilah placed her hands around her coffee cup and inhaled the dark brew. "You are thinking too deeply about what happened yesterday."

His forehead still furrowed, Robert shook his head. "I'm upset I called that one so wrong. I should never have agreed to Barrick. I knew he didn't like Evan. A lot of the crafters think he's jealous of Evan, and they don't hang around him."

"No one knew Barrick would show up on site to steal." Barrick was a grown man. It didn't matter whether he was born in the town or on the edge of town; he was still a responsible adult. Everyone got jealous;

it didn't mean Barrick could resort to stealing. Unfortunately, she didn't think Robert was ready yet to listen to those words.

"The police told me Barrick had other citations," he said as he buttered himself another biscuit. "I don't want the crafters to get a bad reputation because of one rogue member."

"Well, one: he's slunk away into the swamp somewhere. Two: you scared me yesterday. I saw you getting closer and closer. I realize now that you knew what you were doing, but at the time, I was scared."

Robert shrugged. "I had to secure Barrick to make sure you were all right."

She patted his hand. "You were amazing, but let's not do that again." When her joke fell flat for him, she tapped his hand. "What's wrong?"

"The problem is, I let myself get pushed into a bad decision."

"At the time, it seemed like the best way to make sure the crafters would get representation. Barrick wasn't even your choice. You wanted Evan, and that's what we have now."

"The problem with Barrick isn't who he is or even that Sandra chose him. The problem here is, I went against my own instincts, because I wanted to make things work no matter what."

"True, and you made a mistake. We all live and learn. It won't be the last time you make an error. What really matters is that we found out the problem before he was teaching and had access to more materials."

"Not listening to my instincts is what galls me."

"Listen, we could list what is wrong with you all day long. Still, it wouldn't change a thing," she said, laughing over her coffee cup.

Robert grinned. "Wow. You could really find enough things wrong with me to fill the day?

I don't think so. I have it on good authority that I must have a lot of good qualities; otherwise, the good woman Delilah Cade would have nothing to do with me."

Delilah laughed, and when he covered her hand with his, she looked at them together.

"Delilah, thank you."

"For?"

"Believing we are worth it. I would have gotten Peaches on my side and waited you out, but it's good that we didn't have to."

Delilah waved him off and offered him some more coffee.

"No. I've seen this trick. Soften them up and then throw them into the oven." He patted his stomach. "I don't want any more coffee, but I'd be honored if my fiancée would accompany me on a walk."

"I don't know." Delilah held out her left hand. "Am I your fiancée?"

"Ah, that metallic show of my affection. I actually planned on giving it to you tonight at the party."

"Oh! I almost forgot about the get-together, with everything else going on."

Robert tapped her nose. "Go. It's the last day everyone will be there, and it'll be our first project together of many of our union."

"Our first?" Delilah went to get her walking sandals.

"Come with me, and I'll tell you all of my plans," he said in the voice of a pirate.

Chapter Sixteen

Cassandra met Delilah for lunch at the Banter House. She had on a pair of shades and a sundress. When Delilah saw her, she laughed.

"Why are you dressed in those huge sunglasses?"

"I'm hoping if I go incognito," Cassandra whispered, "you'll be able to tell me the skinny on the rumors I've heard since yesterday."

"What rumors might those be?"

After looking over both of her shoulders, the younger woman pulled her glasses down the bridge of her nose to see Delilah. "There was a rumor that Robert saved you like a damsel in distress." She wiggled her eyebrows. "He beat a man who was intent upon manhandling you and then subdued him with lightning reflexes."

Delilah covered her mouth to stop her shout of laughter from disturbing the other people eating in the restaurant. "Oh, my goodness. Is that what's going around? It hasn't even been twenty-four hours."

Cassandra took off the glasses and put them on the table. "I used to live in the city that never sleeps. City folk don't realize small towns not only don't sleep, but they have a twenty-four seven rumor mill that doesn't stop even when there aren't any rumors."

Both of the women laughed. The waitress brought them two lemonades.

"But seriously, I'm not going to let you out of this booth until I hear what is going on between you and Robert."

"Cassandra, I don't think—"

"Before you give me the company line about not telling, just consider I was the one who got the paint and helped you with the trellis. Surely, after trellis painting, we have to be close friends."

Delilah laughed. "When you put it that way...."

"I'd put it any way that would get you to spill."

Holding up her hands, Delilah gave in. "Fine, I'll spill."

"In the last episode I watched, Clarissa had thrown in a monkey wrench, and you were going to tell Robert you were sorry. So, what happened after that?"

Delilah shook her head. "Well, I didn't find him. Instead, I got custody of Peaches, and then I went to work, because I wanted to find him, but he avoided me. At any rate, a crafter named Barrick broke into my building, Robert came to save me, we finally talked, and we made up at the end."

"The end? Are you two getting married?"

Delilah shrugged. "I discreetly asked him for my ring, and he said it was coming."

Cassandra's mouth gaped. "That's it? Wow. So anti-climatic. Now you two are a real couple?"

Delilah brightened. "Yes, we are. So, quid pro quo."

Cassandra's face fell, and she looked sad. "Unfortunately, I don't have the same thrilling news to report."

"What happened?"

"In truth, Delilah, I don't know. I went to see Evan on the outskirts of town. There was a huge party. Almost every crafter attended. At any rate, we ate, we danced, and then in front of everyone, he gave me a bracelet he'd made."

Cassandra held out her hand so Delilah could see the bangle.

"It's gorgeous."

The younger woman nodded. "It's made all from wood, and each bead is actually a ball within a ball with different shapes. I don't know how he made it, but it must have taken forever for him to get the beads done, strung, and then put this amazing lock on it as well."

"Okay, he takes you to a huge party. He gives you jewelry, and then?"

"Then he just stops calling me. When I see him in the street, he nods, but doesn't really acknowledge me. I have to tell you, it's almost embarrassing." She sniffled. "Really, I should have known better. It's not like he said he wanted to date me or anything."

Delilah couldn't put together the actions she was hearing with the Evan she knew.

Changing the subject, Cassandra brightened.

"So, does this mean you and Robert will need a chaperone, so nothing happens before the wedding?"

Delilah laughed. "We have the benefit of age. We can control our hormones."

Cassandra didn't look like she was buying it. "I don't know about that. I read in a magazine just the other day that people in the over-sixty groups are dating and doing all sorts of twenty-something activities."

"I'm not saying I couldn't do those things; I just choose not to."

"At any rate, I wish you and Robert the best."

"Thanks. There's going to be a party tonight, since we've finished the project. Do you want to come?"

Cassandra shook her head. "It seems like a closed thing—"

"If you come, then I'll have an excuse to

leave early. Come on. Go with me?" Delilah smiled at her. "You know you want to."

Cassandra laughed. "Fine. I'll go with you, because I have a dress I've been dying to wear, and I've had nowhere to wear it."

"Whatever the reason, it doesn't matter to me. I'll just be glad that you'll be there."

———

Delilah had picked out a maroon, off the shoulder dress with three-quarter sleeves and a hemline that fell right below her knees. She had matching pumps to go with the dress. While it was a bit daring in fit, she'd give it a one-time shot. She had gone to the hairdresser earlier, and the woman had accented her layers. Delilah's hair felt light and silky.

The evening had already started out with some hiccups. Peaches' sitter cancelled, so Delilah had to take the dog to a boarding house. When she got to the boarding house, they almost didn't take Peaches because they were scared of her.

The staff looked at Peaches and then back at Delilah.

"You said Peaches, so we assumed you had a toy breed."

Delilah shook her head. "Look, she's a senior dog. Can you take her for two nights or not? I hate to be a pain and press this, but if you aren't going to be able to do it, I have to make some quick arrangements right away."

The staff told Delilah to take Peaches into what they called the run room. She placed the pit bull in the room and then said bye. The owner of the house asked Delilah to stay to see how Peaches did. After twenty minutes and all of the staff being able to go in and play with the dog, the owner agreed to take Peaches for the two days.

Robert had arranged to pick her up and bring her to the party, but he called and said that Cassandra would be driving her instead. Delilah was a little disappointed, but decided she'd tell him when she got there, given they were telling each other the truth from now on.

When Cassandra rang the doorbell, Delilah picked up her beige clutch and her matching pearl wrap and went to the door. Cassandra stood outside in a simple black dress with a red flower at the hip. The material was smooth, and the dress fell right below the knees, but Delilah could see all the curves Cassandra normally hid under baggy clothes and blue jeans.

"You look amazing!"

"You look fantastic."

They complimented each other at the same time. When they had finished oohing and ahhing over the dresses, they got into Cassandra's sports car.

"I take it you didn't buy this while you were in Sweet Blooms?" Delilah asked.

Cassandra smirked. "This is a holdover from a life I used to have. I just didn't have the heart to give it up."

When both of them were in the vehicle, Cassandra looked to her side and told Delilah to buckle up.

"I have a feeling I may need to," Delilah said.

"Don't worry. I have a rule: I don't let the baby out unless I'm in the car by myself," Cassandra said.

The drive to the Cade farm took only a few minutes. The farm had been transformed into a dream. White lights in circles like Japanese lanterns lined the paths. As Cassandra and Delilah walked to the main building where music was playing, they passed by the lake. Someone had set at least thirty tea lights on the water, making it look ethereal as they passed.

When they got to the main building, Cassandra opened the door. The smell of food wafted out and pulled Delilah in. A momentary hush fell over the room. After she stepped in, everyone cheered. Cassandra came in, clapping as well.

Robert walked up to her and kissed her on the cheek.

"I want you to know I am a man of my word." Then he turned her around to look at the door. The whole doorway was decorated like a huge trellis.

Facing him, she laughed. "That's cheating. Everyone has walked through this door, not just me."

He brushed his lips over her forehead. "It's true; we all walked through, but it wasn't until you walked through that it mattered and we celebrated. In case I haven't said it with all the things that have been going on: I love you."

Delilah blinked back happy tears. "No, you hadn't said it, but I thought you might have some feelings going that way."

Robert stepped back and patted both his right and left pockets. "Oh, yes. We can't forget the metal token." He pulled out a ring. The setting had one diamond, and the band of yellow and white gold was woven like a Celtic cross. It was beautiful. The thought that went into it as well as the simple design were everything she wanted.

Robert picked up her hand and kissed it. Then he placed the ring on her finger.

"I'm happy you came to your senses and decided to take a chance on me," he said, laughing.

"I'm glad you gave me the time to get past my fears and decide what I was going to do. I don't know that I would have been that patient," Delilah said.

"You are, and always will be, worth every minute. Let's go over here; we have a cake to cut, and we have some bets to pay out."

"Really?" Delilah said.

Robert pointed to the side of the room. All along the wall were the crafters.

"All of them bet that I wouldn't be able to win your heart. Only Evan had any faith in this process. I'll be introducing you to each crafter, and the money will be a donation to the shelter, in honor of Peaches."

Delilah smiled at Robert. "In case I have been remiss, Mr. Parker, I love you too."

The End

Thank You!

If you enjoyed this book, you could check out some of my other series:

Love Happens series. Sweet, small-town romances that show love could be waiting for you right around the corner.

Love Endures series. Clean and Wholesome love doesn't just happen in small towns. It can happen in cities too. Second-chance love stories that prove love endures.

Silver Fox series. Love comes to us in all stages of life. Celebrate the couples who find life after their kids have grown up and sometimes even after their first loves have passed.

Love Saves series. Sweet romantic comedy where couples find out what really matters in their lives, how opposites can do more than just attract, and how love can save us all.

If you have enjoyed reading this book, please take a moment to write a review.

Sign up to my newsletter to receive updates on new releases and promotions.